If you want to be on our confidential mailing list for our Readers' Club Magazine (with extracts from past and forthcoming titles) write to:

SILVER MOON READER SERVICES

Shadowline Publishing Ltd
No 2 Granary House
Ropery Road
Gainsborough
DN21 2NS
United Kingdom

telephone: 01427 611697
Fax: 01427 611776

NEW AUTHORS WELCOME

Please send submissions to
Silver Moon Books
PO Box 5663
Nottingham
NG3 6PJ

Silver Moon is an imprint of Shadowline Publishing Ltd
First published 2007 Silver Moon Books
ISBN 9781-904706-519

THE VICAR'S DAUGHTER

AND DEAR JOHN

TWO NOVELLAS

BY

RICHARD GARWOOD

ALSO BY RICHARD GARWOOD
PAIN ORDAINED

THIS IS FICTION - IN REAL LIFE ALWAYS PRACTISE SAFE SEX!

THE VICAR'S DAUGHTER

There was something odd about this. There was light coming through the shutters. The shutters? I didn't remember being in a room with shutters. Still, the bed was very comfortable. It didn't feel like an ordinary mattress. It was very soft, like the pillow, and it was heaped round me instead of being flat. Perhaps it was memory foam. No, that was impossible because I could get hold of a handful of it and it was soft and yielding in my grasp. For some reason I was convinced that this was a feather bed. I'd never slept in a feather bed. Over me was what felt like a large soft duvet, except that this wasn't like my duvet. I must have been in someone else's house. But whose? It was very quiet. I enjoyed a stretch. Oh! I didn't seem to be wearing a nightdress or pyjamas. How did I come to be in this bed, naked? Where were my clothes? There was a wardrobe. I slipped out of the bed to see if my clothes were in it. I supposed I must have had too much to drink the previous night and someone had brought me home and put me to bed.

There were clothes in the wardrobe, but I didn't think any of them were mine. I found a red jersey skirt with beads hanging from the waist band and a white blouse with long sleeves and a mandarin collar. I was in luck, they fitted me. Even so, I didn't find any underwear. I opened a drawer to find shoes. The only ones that fitted me was a pair of slippers with a low heel. I would have settled for a dressing gown, but there didn't seem to be one there. I turned to back away from the wardrobe and saw that there was a mirror inside the door. I looked back at the reflection of myself. I didn't recognise this girl. I have below shoulder length curly black hair. This girl had very short blonde hair. I gasped. Surely someone hadn't cut off my hair? My eyebrows were quite thick, but these were a slender curve. There was something reminiscent about my eyes, but my lips were fairly ordinary, whilst this girl's lips were very full and perhaps were evidence of a sensuous disposition.

I hadn't buttoned the blouse, so I opened it to reveal as beautiful a pair of breasts as I remembered seeing. I was pleased to see them, and cupped them in my hands. These were definitely bigger and heavier than I remembered mine being and the nipples had gold thread cones screwed on to them. I touched them and it made me shiver. There were curious lines across my skin. I began to wonder what was me and what was someone else and how I had come by these changes. I lifted my skirt in the expectation of encountering a fine bush of luxuriant fleece, but there was nothing covering my pussy. It was completely bare and as I moved I could see more lines and something glittered. There was a small gold bar inserted in each of my sex petals. I touched them to see what I could feel, and the bars seemed familiar, though I had never even had my ears pierced.

I was lost. I knew who I was, but I didn't recognise myself. I went to the windows to open the shutters, but the windows wouldn't open. I looked at the door next to the wardrobe and reached for the handle. It turned readily enough and the door opened. This was not the way out, but a door into a bathroom. I felt it might be a good idea to wash and use the facilities. The floor was warm marble and I sensed under floor heating. There was no window, but an extractor fan whirred into action as soon as I touched the light switch. There was a pile of white towels. There was a bath, a bidet, a loo and a separate shower cubicle as well as a sink with a big bathroom cabinet over it. It had a mirror front and I stared back at what I took to be myself. I opened the door and there was a toothbrush, toothpaste, a hair brush and plenty of moisturisers, shampoos and body creams. No make up, just as in the bedroom.

I took off my clothes, hung them on the door and stepped into the shower. For a moment I looked for a shower cap, but with hair as short as this, I really didn't need to bother. I set the shower to medium hot and water cascaded over me. There was a bar of expensive soap and I used it to cover myself in suds which quickly washed off. My skin seemed to have a light tan all over, which in February was a surprise to me as I avoided sunbeds. I reached between my thighs with the soap and suddenly felt something quite alien inside me. I parted my labia and look down to discover that my clitoris had a thin gold ring piercing it. I was amazed. It didn't hurt, but it must have been agony at the time it was inserted. I touched it with my forefinger and at once I felt myself light up. I thought that I'd better be careful. This little ornament seemed to have done something for my libido. I could feel my breasts go heavy and my nipples became erect. If that is what happened with one touch, I wondered what the outcome of any prolonged manipulation might be. Enough to blow my head off, or get me into serious trouble.

I stepped out of the shower and dried myself with a couple of the towels. It was time for positive action. The strange thing was that I felt happy within myself. I should have been terrified that someone had stolen either my body or my mind, but my mind seemed quite easy and I liked this somewhat more voluptuous version of my body. In fact, as I looked at myself in the mirror I could have quite fancied this good-looking girl, except that I was not that way inclined. I realised there was no point in wondering how I got here, and every point in finding out how I could get back to my home and to work. I was not in a hurry because I got a sudden flash of insight that I was on holiday. I thought I wouldn't worry about where I was or how I came there. But I began to worry that I had lost a lot of memory, particularly of recent days.

I walked about the bedroom naked for a while. I caught sight of myself in the open wardrobe door. I was becoming accustomed to the slightly different balance of my body. My breasts were definitely larger, my waist a size smaller and my buttocks even more perky and rounder than I seemed to recall. I was not used to walking about nude, or looking at myself without my clothes. I was fascinated by the gold cones and the uncovered cleft between my thighs with its golden ornaments. I had heard the girls at the finishing school talk about what a woman could do to herself for her own pleasure, but I had never tried it. Not only did I consider it a sin, but also I was afraid that my mother might have caught me. The bathroom door at home was never bolted and my mother had a habit of coming in to see me when I was in bed to make sure I was alright and kiss me goodnight. In this new freedom I pushed a gentle finger between my furled pussy lips and again encountered the ring. I ran my finger round it until it came full circle and touched the little nub of pleasure. The contact made me draw in my breath and for a moment I choked. Then a careful pressure and an up and down movement over the piercing gave me a thrill which was like the beginning of the descent on the Big Dipper. I felt my throat contract in sympathy with my pussy. The walls of my vagina pulled together as if they were looking for something to hold on to. I sat on the edge of the bed opposite the wardrobe door and opened my legs. The gold in my lips and the ring in my clitoris twinkled in the light. I opened my petals as far as I could with my left hand whilst I laid my first two right hand fingers against my clitoris. Almost at once I felt sensations of delight which infiltrated every part of my body. I began to cough and breathe erratically. I could feel my heart beating wildly. I clasped my breast with my left hand and squeezed it, feeling I needed to get my fingernails between the gold cones and the flesh behind them and pull and pinch and tweak. The thought alone was enough and I was overtaken by what I had seen described as an orgasm. It swamped me. I looked at my face and body in the mirror and wished that there was a man standing between my thighs, doing more to me than I ever could imagine. I started to come down from the climax and I saw that I had expelled a little of my juices onto the rug. I was mortified, but I could think of nothing that I could do about it. I decided it was time to dress and explore.

Having dressed myself as well as I could I made a tour of the bedroom and found an almost concealed door handle among the rich panelling of the lower part of the wall. Did I dare to turn the handle? Why ever not? I took a deep breath and turned and pushed, except that although the door handle turned the door didn't open. It took a moment for me to realise that the door opened inwards. I slipped out of the door and found myself in a long corridor. In the distance at one end I could see lights and the sound of many voices. This just had to be a hotel. I hoped that they would understand my questions when I arrived at Reception. I had a nagging thought that I had come out with very little money and I might not be able to pay the bill. The corridor had a thick red carpet down the centre and doors leading off it on both sides. In between there were pictures which were quite difficult to make out in the subdued lighting. As I progressed down the corridor the pictures became clearer and suddenly I was brought up short by the subject matter of a large square canvas in an elaborate gilt frame. I could not believe the picture. It showed a girl in a red skirt and white blouse being pursued by a number of dogs with several men in elaborate uniforms mounted on horse back following the chase. There was something familiar about the girl. I stared at the picture with my heart beating faster and tightness in my throat. The girl was the image of the new me. I looked to my right, back where I had come from. There was another picture of much the same scene, except that the dogs had gained on the girl. Beside a door I found a light switch and pressed it. A soft light permeated the corridor. Things looked quite different. I realised that I had failed to notice the number on the door of the room I had vacated, which would make it difficult for me to explain my situation to the receptionist. I began to retrace my footsteps in the hope that I might have left the door slightly ajar.

As I walked slowly back down the corridor I looked at the pictures on my left side. They successively depicted the closeness of the dogs. Then one had jumped forward at my running figure and had almost managed to sink his teeth in me. I hesitated before looking at the next picture. This showed the leading dog with a length of red material in his mouth and my skirt torn from hem to waist band. The expression on my face was of terror. The next picture showed another dog who had leapt at me and had torn a panel out of my blouse. My hands were thrown out from my body as I ran but it seemed I had no chance of out-distancing the dogs. The next picture showed a dog in the act of leaping at my back and seizing my blouse in its teeth. I wondered if he had torn my skin, but in the next picture I was revealed, naked to the waist, with a dog either side of me tearing at my skirt. I supposed that I realised that the next picture would be just a progression of myself running terrified and naked from the dogs and the horsemen, but instead it showed me bending to pick up a stout stick as I ran, and I was not quite naked. Drawn up my hips was a jewelled thong whose slender tape between my buttocks was too narrow to be anything other than a means of securing the tiny pad of glittering material at the front.

I had taken a stand in a not very advantageous place in the next picture, and I swung the stick like a club to ward off the dogs. They had fallen back, sensibly deciding that this was a dangerous foe, but I seemed not to have noticed the two dogs which had left the pack and were circling round towards my back.

The next picture showed a melee with dogs falling to the flying stick whilst I was being toppled by the rush of the two dogs against the backs of my legs. I was fearful of the content of the next picture, since I expected to see my savaged and bleeding body being torn to pieces by the dogs. I plucked up the courage to look and found that picture showed the riders, one of whom had my body across the pommel of his saddle with my arms and legs drawn together with a cord tied to them running under the horse's belly.

I could not understand what this meant. How could all these pictures of me have been painted so quickly? A hundred questions flooded into my mind. I was conscious that I had no underclothes beneath my skirt, let alone an elaborately-jewelled thong. I looked for another picture, but though there was a frame after the next door, the canvas was blank. I looked at the door and realised that it was the one that I had opened to come out into the corridor. It had a number on it in Roman figures, CCCXLIII. Surely it would have been easier to use Arabic numbers and just put 343 on the lintel? I was concerned about the pictures, but I turned my head to look at those on the left hand wall, when the light went out. I felt I had to hurry to the end of the corridor. I expected there to be lifts when I emerged into a big landing, but there was only wide flights of stairs. The one nearest me went down, whilst the furthest flight ascended. I reached for the polished brass hand rail and began to make my way down. The hubbub became louder as I descended, but there was a 180 degree turn in the stairs so that all I could see was a blank wall with a huge picture on it. I was about halfway down the stairs when I realised that the picture was of a mounted figure, similar to those in the smaller canvases in the corridor, thrusting a lance through the throat of a fire-breathing dragon who had presumably been decoyed to his execution by the chained sacrifice of a naked girl. I saw that this two and a half metre high figure was another depiction of the revised image of me. Wherever this might have been they certainly didn't seem to be short of talented painters.

I turned the bend of the stairs and before me was a very large chamber with columns supporting the ceiling and numerous people thronging the open spaces. For some reason I kept my eyes fixed on the staircase until I was on the floor with the crowd. I raised my eyes and saw that many of those nearest to me were replicas of myself. For a moment I feared that I had been cloned, but I knew that I was still me, whatever the changes in my appearance might indicate.

There were people doing strange things to one another. On my left there were two replicas of me dressed in purple satin pyjamas who were reclining on a settee. They were in a close embrace and were kissing each other long and deep, whilst their hands wandered over each other's bodies. I realised that if I concentrated hard I could feel the sensations that they were feeling. I blushed and became quite breathless with my breasts tingling. I was getting warm and damp between my thighs.

Normally I don't have very much empathy with other people. I suppose that a word that comes from the Greek for 'passion' would rather rule me out. I don't have much in the way of experience of passion, either. Nonetheless, there I stood, ignored by everyone, watching them and beginning to feel what others feel. This was all a very new experience. I walked round to the left and found another tableau. Here there was a 'me' dressed in what I usually wear, a pair of jeans and a shapeless jumper. This one was talking to a young man and seemed to be keeping her distance. Whoever designed this scene must know me very well. I always keep my distance, especially with good-looking young men. Don't ask. It's just that I feel that Daddy wouldn't approve, and I am certain that Mummy wouldn't.

Listening in to someone else's conversation is not a thing I like to do, so that I moved on to the next group. This was a little group who were having a picnic. There were two men, both young, one fair and clean shaven, the other was dark and sported a beard. The two girls were both 'me' but very differently dressed. One had an off the shoulder blouse with small cuffs which could fit anywhere between her shoulders and her elbows. She seemed to have pulled the blouse down to take advantage of the sun. There was a good deal of cleavage on view and as she sat her skirt had ridden up to her knees, which were raised with her feet apart. From where I was standing I had an excellent view of the gold jewellery glinting between her thighs. She was staring into the eyes of the fair-haired young man. Even from this distance I could feel the tension between them and I knew that he wished to take her breasts in his hand and slip his fingers between her thighs. She reciprocated his thoughts, but as with all human communication there was hesitation between them, in case they were misinterpreting the signals. I realised that I was willing there to be more action in this tableau, so I turned to the other two.

The girl was dressed in something gauzy and clinging, in a mix of pale pink and light green. The dress did almost nothing to conceal her body. She was leaning against the man's raised knee with a hand on his thigh. He had put an arm round her waist and the back of his hand was pressed against the underside of her breasts. He was bent slightly forward from the waist and at first I thought he was whispering something to her. Closer attention showed that his lips were on her skin at the nape of her neck and he was running a line of kisses along the bare skin where the neck of her dress was open. I could feel her shiver with delight and I knew that she wanted him to move his hand so that it would cup her breasts. She showed distinct signs of being interested in being seduced. My immediate thought was that she should be careful, but then, she was apparently feeling things from the man that I had never yet felt.

The figures in each of the tableaux seemed to be stuck at a particular point in their relationship. The next group was entirely unexpected. There was another 'me', but this time she was not enjoying herself. A seated man had her caught across his thighs and was holding her neck with one large powerful hand. Meanwhile his other hand was being applied with some strength to her bottom which was encased in white, close-fitting panties. She was kicking her legs and shrieking, but the punishment was inexorable. I concentrated on her and realised that she was thinking that this was something that she would remember all her life. She also seemed to feel that it was worthwhile to endure a little pain in order to get this very close attention. I knew how she felt. I did anything to get my Daddy's attention, but somehow my Daddy always seemed to ignore my attempts to get him to take an interest, and even resorting to what I considered to be extremes of naughtiness brought me no more than a reprimand from my mother.

I thought this girl was luckier than me. Somebody cared so much that they exposed her pretty buttocks and they were being ruthlessly smacked. I tried to tune into her mind, which at first was total confusion, but then her thoughts and feelings became clearer. She was rebelling against the steady rise and fall of the large hand. The impacts were painful. She felt degraded by her position lying across the man's knees and held down so that she couldn't move. Tears sprang from her eyes and her mouth uttered incoherent sounds, whilst she kicked ineffectually with her legs. Then I noticed an overlay of other thoughts. 'He is holding me captive. He can do whatever he wants with me. He is so much stronger than I am. I can feel my breasts pressed against his thigh. I wonder if he can feel them and what effect they might have? He can see the outline of my bottom. I want him to pull down my briefs and smack me so that his fingers contact my pussy. I want....oh, I want....please do something to me.'

I was amazed that the degradation caused her by the punishment should be associated with a desire to reveal her most secret places. It was not at all clear to me just what it was that she wanted. I could feel her unfamiliar warmth between her thighs communicated to me very clearly. But then I wondered what could it all mean? I spent several minutes observing the action, but like the other tableaux there seemed to be no progression in the action despite the passage of time. Her bottom stung, she still desired more, but nothing further was forthcoming.

I liked the look of the next group very much. There

was a slender but muscular tanned young man wearing nothing but a pair of tight black jeans lying on top of a big bed and holding another 'me' in his arms. He kissed her from time to time and her fingers stroked his face and his chest. She was wearing a pale blue dress with buttons from the neck to the hem. A fair number of the top buttons were undone and I could see the substantial swell of her breasts quite largely uncovered and, as she turned closer towards him her breasts pressed against his chest. He began kissing her with his mouth open, pushing his tongue into her mouth and questing within her. I could see the rapid increase in the speed of her breathing which I thought must be echoed by the speeding up of her pulse. It was time to tune in.

I seemed to have learned something from each of these tableaux, but I had not, so far, been able to tune into the mind of anyone but 'me'. Here was another case when what I tuned into was not quite what I expected. This girl was loving every moment of being held close to the young man's body. His kisses were lighting her fires, or rather they were making little electric trickles which ran down her throat to her body. I sensed her heart beating as if she had just run several hundred metres and her breath coming in gulps between his penetrating kisses. The overwhelming sensation I gathered from her was her desire to explore his body and give herself to the man who was holding her. It was unclear exactly what she wanted to do, but as I stood before them and watched her fingers stroke his belly, I was conscious that she wanted to undo the leather belt which was tight around his hips, pull down the zip and discover whatever it was that was hidden beneath the black denim. I couldn't get any sort of complete image of what she hoped to find, and it wasn't clear what she would at once do with her discovery. At the same time she was willing him to undo more of her buttons and lay her breasts bare and then pursue his own exploration until all her buttons were undone and he could put his hand between her thighs. This gave me a distinct shock and I uttered a tiny cry. It could have been as loud as I liked, because it seemed no-one took any notice of me or could see or hear me, but merely got on with what they had been doing when I arrived. This girl was melting with desire and I had a feeling that the young man was as keen on carrying forward their passion as she was, but the action got no further than when I first encountered them. I turned away, wondering what I might have done if this had really been me. I was sure that it would have gone no further than they had managed. My parents had brought me up to be extremely modest and careful. The scenes played out before me were a revelation, though I had to admit, not a completely unpleasant one.

After all, these girls were not me, just as much as I was not. I wondered for a

moment what this meant until I realised that I was able to identify fully only with a girl who

had dark hair and the features with which I was familiar. The girl I was now had my values

and experiences, but these were not shared by the girls I was observing.

I was impelled to go on to the next tableau. At first I could not understand this one at all. There was what looked like a boxing ring. In one corner there was my clone. In the other was a girl with copper-coloured hair and penetrating green eyes. They were dressed in sleeveless crop tops which came just below their nipples, leaving much of the lower halves of their breasts exposed. Apart from that they were wearing G-strings, whose straps disappeared into the cleft between their buttocks. The rest of their bodies were without any covering. I have never revealed as much of myself to anyone else as these two were doing.

A man was standing in the centre of the ring and obviously announcing something. I at once tried to tune into my double, but was only able to connect with fear and fury.

There was some sort of signal and the two girls moved to the centre of the ring. The redhead made a lunge, but the blonde girl caught her arm and twisted her round off balance. The redhead's flailing arm sought for something to get a grip on and her fingers encountered the strap of the blonde's crop top. She used this to steady herself as they both remained on their feet, but the blonde girl took the arm she was holding up the redhead's back and began to force her head and the upper part of her body down. The redhead had not disentangled her fingers from her opponent's crop top but it must have been tough material because it didn't tear, but it did stretch and hung loose over her shoulder and down her chest revealing the upper part of her breast on that side in the process. This didn't seem to be much of an advantage to the redhead so she let go and without warning dropped to her knees, pulling the blonde with her. The blonde let go of the redhead's arm with one hand and put her arm out in front of her to avoid doing a somersault over her opponent's shoulder. At once the redhead twisted out of the blonde's grasp and threw her off her back so that she landed with her body sprawled, face up on the mat. Before she had a chance to collect herself the redhead was kneeling over her, holding her arms down. At this point the blonde was looking distinctly dishevelled with her crop top askew and one breast completely uncovered. She began to kick her knees up in an attempt to strike the redhead on the back and push her off, but the redhead simply moved forward over the blonde's body until she was able to trap the blonde's biceps with her knees. She now had both hands free to do as she wished and promptly raised her bottom so that she could get a grasp on the blonde's crop top which she dragged over her breasts and then her head, doubling it round her neck and armpits. The blonde was now, to all intents and purposes, naked to below her waist, an image which I found disturbing. I tuned in to find that the blonde was concentrating her mind on how to free her arms and gain some advantage on her adversary. The redhead had the blonde's nipples in her fingers and was pulling and twisting them mercilessly. She appeared to think that she had won and was cruelly delighting in the discomfiture of her opponent.

I registered the pain and humiliation that the blonde was suffering, and also a slight overlay of pleasure at the presence of her almost naked opponent and a curious desire to relax into the pain of the attentions to her breasts. For several seconds it seemed that she was prepared to try to enjoy what the redhead was doing. But that was hardly the way to come out even, let alone win. Suddenly she made a great effort, arching her back and forcing down on her bent knees at the same time twisting her body so that the redhead fell to her side and released her grip both on her arms and her nipples. The redhead was first on her feet, the blonde lunged forward with both arms as if to grasp her opponent by the waist, but the redhead turned abruptly and the blonde's hands slid down the redhead's sides. For a moment it seemed as if this was a defeated tactic, but as the redhead moved away from the blonde her G string was engaged by both the blonde's hands. Before she could do anything about it the quite fragile tape had parted and the blonde dragged the thong down the redhead's legs to below her knees. The redhead made a futile grasp for the scrap of covering, but at once realised that it was torn and unusable and instead covered herself between her thighs with her hand. The blonde threw herself at the redhead's thighs grasping them in a bear hug, preventing her from moving and causing her to bend at the waist. The redhead needed something to stop her toppling over backwards so she in her turn grasped the blonde's G-string tape. Either the blonde's tape was considerably stronger, or the angle was wrong. The tape didn't break, but was drawn sharply between the blonde's legs. Meanwhile she was bearing all her strength towards the redhead, and having her legs free she sought to topple her opponent.

Sweat was running off both their bodies which were becoming slippery. The blonde's feet scrabbled for purchase on the canvas floor as she pushed hard against her opponent. The redhead caught her by her short hair and pulled her head up, but she was overwhelmed by the pressure on her thighs and fell backwards with a howl and a thump. The tableau was now the reverse of the earlier one. This time the blonde was astride the redhead, sitting across her belly. She managed to capture the redhead's left arm with her right hand and pressed it down to the canvas. The redhead swiftly evaded the blonde's attempts to trap her right arm and in so doing slapped the blonde's breasts with her right palm. The blonde uttered a cry of fury and redoubled her efforts, but in so doing she paid less attention to the trapped left arm than she should have done. In an instant the redhead tore her arm free and inserted the fingers of both hands in the blonde's G string, giving it a violent tug which this time broke the tape which was securing it. At the same time the blonde reached forward to the redhead's crop top and exerting all her strength tore it down from the top seam. The redhead managed to roll away from the blonde and backed into a corner of the ring.

At this stage the blonde sought to pull her top down over her breasts, but finding this was impossible she pulled it over her head. The redhead divested herself of the remainder of her own top and I had a perfect view of the whole of her beautiful body with its round, firm breasts, erect nipples, curved belly and the thin covering of auburn fleece between her thighs, trimmed so that the fold of her lips was clearly visible. Apart from myself I had never seen a woman naked before and I took in this lovely creature with a mixture of aesthetic delight and then what I realised must be lust. I wanted to be her opponent, though I doubted if I might have had the equanimity to stand before her, naked.

The two naked girls began to crouch and look for an opening in the other's defences. The green eyes sparkled, but I was able to tune in to the blonde who, to my surprise, clearly wanted to do something to the redhead which wasn't completely formed in her mind. Both girls were panting and their bodies were slick with their own and the other's sweat. Suddenly there was a flurry of movement and the two bodies came together. Each had her arms round the other's chest and was squeezing in a bear hug, breast to breast. As their feet moved I realised that both of them were trying to throw the other by tripping her up. A sort of malicious dance proceeded in which sweat mingled with sweat and one body pressed against the other.

Before there was any outward sign of who was achieving a breakthrough the redhead toppled backwards with the blonde on top of her. In her fall the redhead had managed to get her left arm under her own back. The blonde was lying between the redhead's legs. Suddenly I received a hot ruby glow from the blonde's mind. She leaned forward, her heavy breasts touching those of the redhead whilst she sank her head towards her opponent.

In a moment the blonde engaged her opponent's mouth with her own and was kissing her. Then I saw her reach between her own legs with her free hand and grasp the redhead's pussy, moving her buttocks up to facilitate her movement. From my viewpoint I could see the blonde's slightly open buttocks displaying the dark pink crater of her nether hole and the entirety of the slot between her thighs. I could also see the blonde's fingers working on the redhead whilst she renewed her deep kisses.

The redhead lay with her arms and legs outstretched, completely at the mercy of the blonde. I looked on in amazement as the redhead began to squirm and lift her buttocks so that the blonde could achieve even deeper penetration. As the blonde took her lips away for a moment I could hear the stertorous breathing of the redhead as she gulped in air and her ribs expanded, visible through her skin. She began to cry out and I watched the blonde's fingers move faster and press harder. As I watched in fascination and some shock at this tableau, I saw that the blonde was weeping little trickles of something juicy from her slot and it was making a trail down her thighs.

Suddenly the redhead arched her body and howled like a dog in pain. The blonde took her hand away and I was able to see the redhead's open pussy with liquid gushing from it. Almost at once the blonde lay down again on the redhead and they held their mouths together. I was depraved enough to wait two or three minutes to see what next might transpire, but my mind was full of the blonde's lust and her desire for power over the redhead in a way which was utterly irresistible. I found that I was shaking and my mouth was dry. I was shocked by what I had seen, none of which I had had any idea was possible for a woman or between women.

Eventually I drifted away from the sight of the blonde's

pert buttocks raised above the redhead and their bodies clamped together in what I took to be a loving embrace. I wondered what I had learned from this tableau, as I was clearly intended to learn something from each of them.

It was not long before I found myself face to face with another scene. There was a strange sort of mistiness between each of the scenarios. The last one seemed to grow smaller very quickly and disappeared into a mist, whilst the next blossomed into view as if a curtain had been very rapidly raised to disclose the scene before me. If I had found the last tableau difficult to take in at first, then this was even more so. Here there was a sizeable pile of logs in a clearing with what looked like a timber shack in the background. A double-headed axe of a sort I had never seen before except in museums devoted to ancient weapons, was leaning against the big lump of wood which I thought might be the chopping block. There were a few bushes at the edge of the clearing and judging by the length of the shadows it was intended to indicate it was midday. I could hear a man's voice, but there was no sign of the speaker, and for once no evidence of the existence of the blonde girl.

Ridiculous as it may sound I thought I ought to stand and watch for a while as otherwise I might be thought to be rude. The fact that I might be missing something hardly occurred to me as my mind was full of the fighters in the previous scene and the pressure they felt to overwhelm and win against a sexual partner. This had nothing to do with romance as I had read about it and had come as something of a shock, particularly in terms of the intimate physical reactions to passion, and that such passion was possible between two women. Whilst I was turning these worrying thoughts over in my mind the man's voice became louder and into the clearing strode a man of middle age and powerful physique dressed like a pastiche of Davy Crockett. I was prepared to snigger to myself but the man exuded power and authority and looked extremely tough to the point of ruthlessness. I had taken no notice of a small heap of hay which lay to the far side of the clearing. The man approached it and uttered a curse. He unhitched a leather strap from his belt and suddenly flailed it down on the far side of the heap. The result was a scream and the appearance of my clone from where I assumed she had been lying asleep.

As she stood up he caught her another slash across her back and she cowered away from him. He pointed at the logs and she skirted round him to approach the heap. I had become used to seeing what I took to be myself in varying stages of dress, but this time I wondered what I had drifted into. An American backwoodsman with a girl. He was dressed in suede, and so was she, except that her suede was little bigger than one of his hands. A flap of leather hung from a cord round her waist to cover her front. As she turned I saw that attached to the back of the cord was a bunch of thistles which chafed her skin as she moved. She was quite heavily tanned by her almost completely naked skin being out in the sun, but even so dark lines ran this way and that across her body, both front and back. This was no loving relationship, she had been beaten hard and often. He flicked the strap at her and struck her voluptuous breasts making her cry out and clasp them in her hands. Another flick and another cry and she picked up a log and balanced it on end on the chopping block.

She grasped the handle of the axe with both hands and swung it up above her shoulder, bringing the blade neatly down on the top of the log and splitting it in two. I watched her carefully. I had seldom seen anyone split logs, other than the old man in the cottage by the wood at home. She seemed too slight to use the heavy axe, but as she lifted it I saw the muscles standing out on her belly, arms and back and I admired the strength in her slender body.

She had obviously had a great deal of practice at splitting logs, for she was accurate as well as fast. I watched the insides of her upper arms push against her breasts as she brought the axe down and they jumped and jiggled, though she seemed unaware of them and the man merely stood to one side watching her work. I wondered what it was I was supposed to learn from this scene. The girl's task seemed mundane and inappropriate. I saw that she was beginning to sweat. I already knew how much women could sweat from the last tableau, though it had been a revelation to me. I realised that I was quite unaware that a sylph like my alter ego could engage in heavy manual labour. I wondered why she should want to. It was time to tune in. My first impression was of intense concentration on the job in hand. The logs had been sawn cleanly and with right angle faces so that, for the most part there was no problem in setting them up on the chopping block. She seemed to be repeating something over and over which I could not quite make out. It sounded like 'Must do this well, must do this well....' but interspersed was another message, 'He will punish me, he will punish me again, I must do this well.' There was an element of panic in her body as she attacked the logs. I wondered how he could punish her if she held a sharp axe which she well knew how to use. I thought that if he tried to punish me I would swing the axe to scare him off.

Then there was the way she was dressed. Alright, it was a warm day, but surely she should have had some proper clothing, if only for the sake of decency. I switched into her mind, she seemed to be muttering some sort of mantra: 'He is the master, I must obey. He is the master, I am his slave.' I couldn't believe it. How could an attractive, intelligent, physically strong girl fall into the ownership of a man? Judging by his clothes I was watching an event sometime in the late nineteenth century. Slavery had been abolished by the middle of the century, and in any case white women were not supposed to be the slaves of white men. Whatever I thought about the matter, her body gave plenty of evidence that she had been treated worse than a farm animal and his expression as he looked at her was one of arrogant indifference. She seemed to have little value to him other than as a worker on his behalf. I continued to watch and noticed that not a word was said between the two of them. He reached in his pocket and produced a flask which he uncorked and raised to his lips. He turned away towards the shack as she continued to split the logs and pile them neatly to dry in the hot sun.

After a few minutes she rested and wiped the sweat from her forehead with the back of her hand. It was the wrong thing to do. The man appeared from the shack and walked up behind her. As she became aware of him she started in a way which could only be prompted by feelings of guilt and at once began to pick up the axe and start chopping again. He shouted something at her which I took to be a complaint that she would work only when supervised. He took the axe from her and walked her to the side of the clearing. He struck her on the side of her face, but she had begun sobbing before the blow was struck. She bent down facing me and was doing something to her feet or ankles that I could not see. She stood facing me with her feet well apart, her head down and her body shaking with her sobs. The man tied her wrists together in front of her and she stood looking the

26

picture of misery. He reached up and caught hold of a dangling rope which he pulled down towards him. He was putting considerable effort into hauling the rope down and it proved to be tied to the upper part of the trunk of a young ash sapling. At an order she raised her hands in front of her and he tied the rope to the cords round her wrists, keeping tension on the rope as he did so. He pulled at the rope which seemed taut and then loosened his grip on it.

Suddenly the girl's arms were dragged upwards by the pull of the ash tree trying to return to vertical. I could see her muscles distending as she tried to control the pull on her body. Her feet had come just clear of the ground where they were tied to hooks in a heavy rock. The slender but confident body had been hauled to a torturous extremity. Her arms looked as if they were being dragged from their sockets. Every rib on her sides stood out as if trying to burst through her skin. Her waist had become dangerously narrow with the distance between the bottom of her rib cage and her protruding hip bones lengthened and her circumference reduced so far that it looked as if she was in danger of being torn in two. Her navel had elongated to echo the lower crease, her legs were taut and quivering under the unrelenting tension of the sapling.

She was moaning from the agony she was enduring, but he stood in front of her and just to one side and I could see the sneer on his profile. This was apparently not enough to satisfy his desire to punish her. He turned towards her and pulled the bow in the cord which held her apron in place. It fell away at once revealing her completely naked. I should have got used to seeing her nude by now, but I remembered each time that I was looking at the new image of myself, and I shared in the feelings which went with my observation of the girl. I

27

found that she was less concerned about being naked than what was to happen to her next. I felt shame that she should have to be tortured by being almost torn apart and apprehensive that more was to come.

He took the bunch of thistles off the cord and them down the ineffectually concealing apron. She was looking at him with undisguised fear. She hadn't long to wait before he swung his arm and slashed her across her breasts with the prickly plants. She emitted a ghastly cry of strangled pain and fear. He ignored her and repeated the blow twice more. Then he stepped forward to stand right in front of her. He put his left hand round the back of her head and I thought he was about to kiss her. So intent was I in looking for this display of affection that I failed to see what his right hand was doing. The screech which came from the girl's mouth was unearthly in its intensity. She cried out as loudly as she could in protest at whatever it was that he had done to her. I wanted to leap into the scene and protect her from her tormentor but something other than cowardice held me back. I tuned in to her and found her full of dreadful anguish emanating from a fearsome pain between her legs. I tried to rid myself of the images and the feelings, but they continued to fill me with pain as he stepped away from her and I saw that he had forced the bunch of thistles between her thighs and that some had penetrated her vulva and must have gone inside her, piercing her delicate membranes and spiking her most grievously. Her beautiful body was seized with fear and agony. Tears streamed down her face. Her moans penetrated my heart. I wanted to cut her down from her rack and soothe her and save her from any further misery. I could willingly have killed the man there and then and such was my emotional state that I attempted to enter the scene to carry out my wishes, not even thinking that if he could so mistreat my doppleganger he would have no compunction about treating me in the same way. I needn't have been concerned, as the moment I stepped forward the scene became misty, the figures seemed to be snatched to a great distance and I was left clutching at nothing.

Despite the disappearance of the two figures and their surroundings, my arms and legs ached, my waist was strangely tender and worst of all there was a dreadful pain between my legs. I had no idea what to do next and stood facing the vanished tableau, gently massaging my arms and attempting to hold the cloth of my skirt away from my belly and the tops of my thighs. My tears echoed hers. My concern for her filled my mind. There was always something to be learned from each of these scenes. I supposed that this time it was something to do with falling under the spell of someone who was indifferent to me. Even if he hated her he might have hurt her grievously, but he would want to be rid of her. Here it seemed that he didn't care whether she stayed or went, but if she stayed he was determined to torment her virtually beyond endurance. Her reaction was to treat him as her master and just to suffer. There had to be more than this to life and then I thought that this was a paradigm of two people bound together in some sort of indissoluble union, the inevitable result being abused and the loss of feeling towards one another and in the end...well it hardly bore thinking about.

As my physical pain and mental anguish subsided I turned away and walked stiffly forwards, expecting the very worst from the next scene, if there was to be one. To my surprise the scene was all too familiar. I was amazed to see the school room in which I was taught in my late teens. The blackboard was facing me and the rows of unoccupied desks reached towards me. Once

29

more, nothing seemed to be happening. I heard a bell ring and the door opened and uniformed girls streamed in. There I was again, but so much changed even from my juvenile self. The mistress followed the children who stood in their desks and wished her good morning. After she replied they sat down in silence waiting for her instructions. These were soon given and files were taken out from bags and pens and pencils were produced. The mistress turned to the blackboard and began to write on it. As she did so there was a murmur of conversation from the class. She at once turned and ordered them to be quiet. Unfortunately the quiet lasted only a minute or two and this time the teacher was looking to make an example. I was not at all surprised when she caught my other half leaning across to a girl in the next row. She was ordered to stand up and get the School Sergeant and his deputy. I could feel the fright that immediately affected the girl. Her legs trembled and her mouth became dry. She pressed her knees together in an urgent attempt to prevent herself from peeing with fear. Whatever the order involved it was clear that she was frightened out of her wits by what was to happen. I recognised the class as being the final year, so they must have been eighteen years of age or thereabouts. Surely nothing too untoward could happen to fully grown young women, most of whom were voting citizens?

She was back quite quickly accompanied by a large, tough-looking man who had all the signs about him of having been in the army. His assistant was very much younger, and was wearing a T-shirt and jeans with thick boots. The teacher told the Sergeant that the girl was to be an example to the other girls that politeness and discipline must be maintained at all times. She said only one word to the unfortunate girl who blushed to the roots of her hair and then reached under her skirt and pulled down her white knickers and stepped out of them, holding them bunched in her hand.

I failed to understand the mistress's next command, which was 'Horse her.' There were gasps from the other girls which presaged the assistant gesturing to the girl to approach him. As she did he turned his back on her and told her to give him her hands. In a moment he had crouched and had drawn her arms over his shoulders until her head was on a level with his own and her body was closely pressed to his back. I could feel the quiver running through the girl's body at being held close to the young man and pressing her breasts, belly and mound against his back. He pulled her up a little further and then stood up. Her feet were quickly off the ground. He then bent forward, still holding her wrists as she sought to get some purchase with her feet to relieve the strain on her arms. Eventually she folded her knees around his hips and hung on tightly. For a moment I thought I detected through the fear a slightly erotic sensation as she gripped the young man's muscular body and pressed herself against him. Whatever she felt it was certain that he was enjoying the close contact with so much that was curvaceous and beautiful.

Once the position was to the mistress' satisfaction she ordered the young man to turn away from the class. She then uttered the single word 'Reveal' and the Sergeant moved towards the pair and caught hold of the hem of the girl's skirt and pulled it up her back. I was presented with the image of the girl's bottom with her legs wide apart and the petals of her sex apparently fluttering, a view shared by every girl in the class. The teacher looked at the Sergeant and told him to strike, slowly. The Sergeant slid a tawse from a long pocket in his uniform trousers and flexed it. He drew back his arm and I felt the girl scream inwardly as she awaited the inevitable slash across her buttocks. What had been inward was soon to become an outward expression of pain and misery at the violation of her perfect globes. The sound of the tawse striking the upper curve of her bottom was like a pistol shot. There was a discernible pause whilst she gathered her breath to scream and I shared with her the fire which burnt into her. I shared too, the glow which her contact with the young man's body, the humiliation of the exposure of her intimate parts to everyone present and, strangest of all, the pain itself was generating. I was moved to slip my hand into the pocket of my skirt and feel myself heated and gently pulsing between my legs.

The second strike crossed the first and left a bright weal, just as the first had done. The girl cried out again and the fire burned as fiercely as the first time. I now noticed that she had moved herself slightly up his body by using her knees and had dropped her face down on to his shoulder. I realised that mine were the only eyes that could see that she was kissing his neck and the curve where his neck joined his shoulder. She was behaving like an adoring lover whilst he trapped her against himself. The third strike was slightly lower on her buttocks and she let out a howl of anguish, cut short only by her mouth sinking onto the young man's shoulder. She seemed to find this intensely erotic as well as a diversion from the pain being inflicted on her. I noticed that her pulse had increased markedly in both speed and power, and that she was becoming distinctly squashy between her thighs, whilst she gasped for breath and gulped it down. The fourth strike caught her low on the buttocks and I was aware from my view of the strike and the shared agony that the tawse had penetrated between her cheeks and had caught her pussy, inflicting excruciating pain and at the same time causing her to raise her head and scream as the blow released something within her that I felt rise up from between her thighs, through her belly and into her chest, where her breathing became difficult as her throat constricted and her mind went into a pattern of bright lights and stars. She found it impossible to keep her grip with her knees and I saw that in her moment of release she had produced a gush of liquid which spread down from her pussy and across the lower part of the young man's back. All the girls could see this sign of passion, but fortunately neither the Sergeant nor the mistress was an observer.

The mistress gave the order to stop and the young man raised the upper part of his body and slowly slipped her arms down so that her feet were touching the floor. Tears streaked her face, and she was shivering and shuddering and apparently involuntarily holding on to the young man's waist as her knees buckled and she looked up into his face with an expression that had in it an element of longing and unfulfilled desire. The Sergeant handed her the knickers which she had dropped and told her to resume her chair. This could hardly have been the most comfortable of venues for her bruised buttocks, but she stumbled to her desk and lowered herself very slowly into it. The young man faced the Sergeant and the teacher and managed to conceal from them, but not from the girls, the evidence of his victim's passion.

The two men left the classroom and the lesson seemed to proceed, though the people in the tableau had frozen into immobility. The mist began to form and the scene dissolved before me. Here was another new experience. I had not realised that there was a hidden pleasure in being stripped and abused and that pain was an aphrodisiac. I suspected that the boy had produced all sorts of hidden stimuli which I should have had to encounter personally to have experienced and understood. I realised how very little experience and understanding I had. But I was learning, though what good it would be to me I had no idea.

I was concerned about how many more scenarios there were to be, what I would learn from each of them and then how I could return to the world I knew as reality in the form to which I was accustomed. I felt that days had passed since I descended the stairs into the hall, but I knew that it was probably only a quite short period of time. I felt neither hunger nor tiredness, only a feeling that I was being stimulated and taught at the same time. I was concerned that all the erotic images were so alien to my understanding of what the world was like. How were they generated? And what should I gain from them? Or, perhaps that wasn't the idea at all and they were just warnings.

As I stood there I heard the sound of music and realised that the voice I could hear was that of Madonna. The song was very much in the tradition of what I had been experiencing during my observation of the scenes. It contained words like 'tie my arms behind my back' and 'whip me' which I found both shocking and stimulating. I wondered if anyone would ever do such things to me and if I could willingly participate. Then it occurred to me that I had seen myself in such situations through the feelings of my doubles, but that they were hardly willing participants, and in any case a girl with short blonde hair and the other personal accoutrements was not me, either as a double or as the myself who stood and watched.

A great many other thoughts dashed confusingly through my mind until I became aware that another tableau was evolving before me. This seemed to be a large, all-purpose room, a sort of loft apartment, which I had seen in some of the more extravagant magazines.

Over on one side was what looked like a cooking area with many built-in appliances? Near that was a long table with six chairs and a carver at each end. There was nothing on the table except an ornate candelabrum with several arms and long red candles in the sconces. Immediately in front of me was a huge fireplace with a long sofa on either side at right angles to the fireplace and a low table between them which had on it several magazines and a magnificent vase filled with brightly-coloured flowers. To the left was a shaded area which seemed to contain a large bed. There were doors off the main area, particularly on either side of the fireplace. There appeared to be a long line of built-in cupboards on the left hand side wall behind the bed. The windows reached from ground to ceiling which was very high. So high that there was a theatre-style lighting grid, which went the full width of the room and was equipped with numerous lights.

The scene showed every sign of the possession and expenditure of considerable wealth. To the left of the fireplace the door opened and my double, followed by a very good looking, strong, healthy young man walked in. She was wearing a very dark red satin jersey dress, cut low and open enough at the front to reveal the whole of the inner curve of her breasts and clinging to every curve of her body without being marred by any untoward seams. She was quite stunningly elegant. She stood straight and smiled at him, her surprisingly dark eyes fringed with long lashes and surmounted by pencil-thin eyebrows. I could see her nipples protruding into the material and so close was the fit that the arch of her rib cage and the swell of her belly were apparent. As she moved the material drifted between her legs and graphically outlined the mound at the top of her thighs. She turned and I saw that the back of the dress was cut even lower than the front and hung over her buttocks like a second skin. She had put her evening bag on the coffee table and as she bent to pick it up the cloth shifted against her skin and hung from just above her buttocks. Wherever she had been I imagined that every heterosexual male would have desired her.

He was in a dinner jacket. It was classically cut and utterly immaculate, but failed to conceal what was obviously an athletic and muscular body which moved with power and grace like an animal at the height of its strength. He was both a foil and a complement to her beautiful poise. It looked as if they had been to a party. He asked her if she had enjoyed it and she turned to him, reached up and put her arms round his neck and kissed his lips. He held her close to him and the clinch lasted several seconds.

It struck me that their polite and courteous dealings with one another were based on respect, affection and a great deal of sophisticated civilisation.

'You're gorgeous, you know that?' he asked her. Her response was to whisper in his ear and he laughed. 'Well, I share your desires,' he replied. 'Shall we have something to drink?'

They settled on a cocktail which he deftly concocted from a number of ingredients whilst she sat on a sofa and put her feet up on the coffee table, having discarded her glittering high-heeled slippers that perfectly matched her dress. He brought hers to her and then sat opposite her. They continued to discuss the earlier part of the evening.

'What did you think of Meriel?' she asked him.

'Well, if she'd been wearing any less I would have thought we'd been invited to an orgy.'

'You certainly spent a lot of time looking at her.'

'There was a lot to see. In any case I noticed that you

were taking a particular interest in her husband.'

'Oh, Richard's such a delight. Did I tell you that he has agreed to publish my next book, and I've hardly done more than rough out the plot so far.'

'What's this one about then?'

'Usual sort of stuff. Quiet girl falls in with romantic, good-looking male who starts to awaken her sexual appetite, but finds keeping her satisfied very difficult, so he imposes his will on her and resorts to all sorts of barbarities, particularly when he finds that she has been getting involved with a professional associate.'

'I see you are writing from what you know. It sounds worryingly like our lives.'

'No one else will know.' She looked at him over the brim of her glass, emphasising her lustrous eyes.

'But what if he marks her?'

'Easy, she just wears concealing clothes for a few days. Or doesn't go out and walk about the house naked, showing off her trophies. The problem is thinking of something which she can do which will excite his just revenge without disturbing the equilibrium of their relationship.'

'She could try fondling her hostess' husband and going out on the balcony so that he can fondle her.'

'You were keeping a close eye on me tonight,' she replied.

'Yes. And you definitely deserve punishment.'

'You wouldn't...?'

'You know I will, and now is the time.' He picked up a remote control from the coffee table and flicked a couple of buttons. There was the quiet hum of an electric motor and very shortly afterwards a bar about a metre and a half in length started to descend from the lighting gantry. It stopped at rather less than two metres from the floor.

'Get up,' he commanded in very much less than his previous civilised tone. She put her empty glass on the coffee table and stood up. But this time facing down and clearly awaiting the next order. I tuned in and registered a mix of apprehension and delight. He was about to punish her and though she feared she might feel pain she was filled with a boiling lust. I couldn't understand the contradictory emotions and had no time to consider the situation as he approached her and she turned her back to him. His hands seemed to be busy at the back of her dress and then he pulled the straps over her shoulders and the dress slithered over her body and rippled into a pool at her feet. She at once adopted the female defensive position with one hand covering the top of her thighs and the other clutching one breast whilst her forearm sought to protect the other.

He seized her by the upper part of her arm and pulled her towards the hanging

bar. I could feel the apprehension stirring in her belly as he pulled her arm up to the bar and clamped her wrist to it. She did not try to resist him as he repeated the work with the other arm. He pulled a leg to one side and lifted a small hoop from the floor and attached her ankle to it, repeating the imprisonment with the other ankle at a distance of half a metre. He slid a fluffy rug between her feet and stood back to admire his work. I was presented with an image of the double of myself of quite startling beauty as she stood spread-eagled in her bonds. He flicked the remote again and the bar rose just enough to put her entire body in tension. I gazed at her wonderful figure. Her breasts started to swell about ten centimetres below the hollow between her collar bones. From that beginning there was almost a straight line moving out from her chest until the nipples protruded, grown tense with excitement. From the nipples there was a wonderful curve back to her ribs, giving fullness and firmness. Her nipples looked slightly outwards from her chest so that one breast was seen almost in profile whilst the other was turned towards me.

The cleft between her breasts was continued in the muscles of her lower rib cage and gave way to the narrowing of her body at her waist. From there her hips spread out on either side of her slightly convex belly with the deep elongated pit of her navel the apex of a line which curved down to the sparse, shorn fleece of her mound and the outer lips of her sex, still neatly furled against one another despite her legs being open. I could see the swell of her haunches matching the indent of her pussy and then her thighs, slender and muscular, pulled apart by the stance which she was forced to adopt. For a moment I thought that this would be no more than a repeat, in a rather more urban and sophisticated form of the scene with the backwoodsman. I was wrong.

Her partner was removing his clothes whilst gazing at her with a mixture of delight and lust. I was right in my estimate of his physique, which was bronzed and brawny as well as being lithe and well-toned. He really was a most delightful specimen of masculinity and I could feel a distinct interest growing in me. I knew that he would fade if I attempted to take any part in the scenario, so I restrained myself and concentrated on looking and as far as was possible, tuning into the girl. He was down to a black thong, but I was to be disappointed that he did not match her nakedness. He reached behind a cushion on the sofa and produced a whip which had a thick braided handle with six or seven long strips of narrow leather each with a knot at the end. He hitched the handle into the upper strap of his thong and approached the hanging girl.

He walked round behind her and put his arms round

her waist and his lips on her shoulder. Very slowly he moved his left hand downwards and his right upwards. He caught hold of her beautiful breast in the palm of his hand and reached for her nipple with his forefinger and thumb. His left hand descended to her pussy and he buried two or three of his fingers inside her. She began to utter little gasps of delight and I registered that practised hands were doing wonderful things to her body which seemed to be jerking and twisting as far as was possible given the constraints on her movement. She turned her head towards his and tried to kiss him, but until he moved she managed no more than a little peck. When he did they locked mouths and he began serious manipulation with both hands. I shivered with the intensity of the feelings that were coming across to me. The sweet smell of sexual arousal filled the air. I could see that she was not far from an orgasm. He must have sensed it too, as he withdrew his hands and stepped back from her. She threw her head back between her arms and cried out 'More,' but there was not to be more of that for the present.

He trailed the long strands of the whip over her shoulder so that they spread over her breasts. He slowly withdrew them as she shuddered involuntarily and flicked them at her buttocks. The little sting caused her to tighten her buttocks and tilt her pelvis thrusting her pussy forward. He continued to play with her, flicking the thongs at her buttocks, the tops of her thighs and her waist and back. She uttered little cries as the strands of the whip struck her skin, but I detected more the feeling of a strange pleasure at this abuse than a cry of resentment or pain. He walked round her flicking her side and then her thighs and her belly, giving one brief cut to her pussy, which made her gasp. He caught her across the waist with a slightly harder strike and then took the whip from left to right across her breasts and returned from right to left.

I could not believe that anyone could wish to hurt those beautiful mounds of flesh, but he seemed to have no compunction and I could see one or two pink dots where a knot had left its mark. Something came across from her that she was waiting impatiently for something to happen, and that she was enjoying the stimulus of the whip. He walked round to her back whilst I took in her reactions, striking her more strongly as he did so. He paused as he stood behind her and seemed to be measuring his distance. He swung the whip in an arc and the strands spread out over her back. She cried out and shook as yet another blow caught her lower down the back and was immediately followed by another across her buttocks. I felt her mind clouding over and the pain suppressing all her other feelings, except that this was not quite as she was feeling it and I was at a loss to know what was moving within her. She stuck out her buttocks invitingly but he saw a chance on which she might not have reckoned and swept the whip up between her knees and thighs. I saw the strands come out from between the front of her thighs and some of them bury themselves in her pussy. My mind was full of sympathy for her, but it appeared to be wasted, because although she screeched and howled she made no attempt to draw her buttocks in so that the target was more difficult to access. He slashed her across the small of her back and before she had time to recover he struck her twice again between the legs. She began to howl and as far as she could, swing in her bonds. He stepped to her side, brought the whip down her back and then moved to face her.

I couldn't believe that he was about to do to the tender flesh of her front what he had just done to her back. Although she was standing up she seemed to be lying in the bonds that held her, with her head right back between her arms and her breasts and hips thrust forward. He looked over her beautiful body and flicked the whip at her belly. She gave a short gasp, presumably knowing that this was just the preliminary to another savage attack. He took up his position to the right of her as I tuned into her again. The thoughts which tumbled out of her amazed me. 'Hurt me, thrash me, strip me naked and show me to anyone's eyes, whip me until I come, oh! Whip me, whip me, whip me...'

She hadn't long to wait. He drew back his arm and then made a curving trajectory with the whip until the thongs spread over her lovely belly, leaving points of bright pink from the knots and weals from the raw edges of the thongs. She cried out a long drawn howl which was abruptly terminated when another strike caught her from her navel to just under her wonderful breasts. She howled and choked as the whipping proceeded. She drew her hips back and thrust out her breasts towards him. He needed no encouragement to spread the biting strands of the whip across them, making them bounce and compress and bounce again. He followed this devastating strike with another across the tops of her legs, where some of the thongs cut her between her thighs and scored her pussy. Her howling was continuous, but it seemed to have taken on a different tone. I opened myself to her and encountered a being filled with pain and with passion boiling between her thighs and mounting into her belly. I gathered that all that was missing for her was an audience. As the apparently unnoticed and unseen representative of the audience I watched her and felt a small proportion of the agony and tumult that was consuming her. I became aware as the thrashing continued that the pain had decreased but that the commotion between her thighs was beginning to take her over.

I was certain that a sheen of sweat had developed on the outer lips of her pussy. I was counting the strikes as he laid them on her skin and she shook and howled. I had got to ten when I saw that she was almost in a state of collapse with her head back as far as it would go between her arms, her howling a guttural moan with her mouth wide open and her eyes tight closed.

I could hear her rasping breathing and the crack of the whip against her body which no longer twisted and turned, but hung almost unfeeling as trails of weals and the red dots from the cuts of the knots spread over her skin. Twelve was a heavy blow to her breasts, she seemed hardly to react, though her moan had changed to cries of 'oh, oh, oh,' repeated again and again as the thirteenth struck. As I watched her I saw that her belly muscles were contracting and that as far as she could she was moving her arms and shoulders to press her breasts together so that the nipples showed straight ahead and the elaborate curves melded together into a glorious pillow of flesh. I watched closely as a flush mounted from her chest towards her neck and she suddenly thrust her pelvis forward so that his fourteenth strike was to her flagrantly thrust-forward pussy and the fifteenth to her breasts. The sixteenth was a strike upwards from the ground between her legs, burying the thongs between her thighs. Her gasps of 'oh, oh, oh...' changed to deeper and louder cries of 'ah, ah, ah,' and I was amazed to see liquid spurt from the now slightly open outer lips of her sex which disclosed the pink fronds within and the prominent nub of her clitoris. He slashed her again between the legs, cutting into her beyond her outer lips and catching her clitoris in a savage embrace. Her cries became almost desperate, but I was aware that it was not the agony of the thrashing which produced them but the beginnings of the release of all her sexual energy in a mighty climax, heralded by the spurt and continued by a stream of juices which poured from her onto the rug between her feet.

He cast the whip away and flipped the remote to lower her enough to take the tension off her body. He was skilled in releasing her, setting free her ankles first and then moving behind her and attending to her left wrist, which left her dangling perilously from just her right wrist, until he deftly caught her round her body with his left arm just under her breasts and lifted her slightly so that he could undo the snap catch which secured her wrist. Her knees buckled, but he had anticipated this and had one forearm under her knees and the other under her arms and picked her up as if she were half the weight she appeared to be.

He carried her to the bed which was in the shadow and laid her down very gently with her bottom on the edge of the bed and her spread knees with his knees between them. He leaned forward and supported his weight on his hands whilst he put his mouth to hers and kissed her gently and sweetly. She began to respond and I saw her left hand tug at his thong and then, for the very first time in my life I had an idea, not only what a climax felt like when it enveloped everything else which we are, but now the sweet desire to be penetrated and to take what it is a man has into one's self.

I could not bring myself to share in their love making and I realised that I was only partly and perhaps dimly aware of what it was they had between them in love and lust and pain and passion, which held them so close to one another. As the scene faded I wondered if I would ever have any of these experiences.

****

I was not at all surprised to find myself in bed. I had my usual pyjamas on, but both the jacket and the trousers seemed to be chilly and more than damp. The bed was a mess of tangled sheets and the duvet pulled right up to my chin. My head was pounding and my eyes were sore and gritty. Well, I had been through a hard night. My chest felt tight and as I lifted my head I began to feel very dizzy. I was disturbed to see both my mother and my father bending over the bed and looking at me with great concern on their faces. Normally my father never came into my room. My mother produced an old fashioned thermometer and pushed it into my mouth. I found I could do no more than lie still and wait to see what would happen next. My mother withdrew the thermometer and looked at it with concern, but suddenly a smile spread across her face. 'Ninety-nine point two,' she announced, 'still high, but so much lower than yesterday. The doctor told me that if this happened the worst would be over.'

There was a rap on the door and a smartly-uniformed young woman came in, followed by another. I suddenly realised how weak I felt and also how uncomfortable.

'Thank you for running the bath, Vicar,' the first woman said. 'We'll see to her now.' My parents disappeared from my view. The bedclothes were abruptly pulled off the bed and I found myself being picked up by the two women who carried me into my bathroom. They stripped off my sodden pyjamas, seated me on the side of the bath and then lowered me into the water. It was warm and scented and buoyant. I lay back and found that the first of the women was turning on the shower attachment and was washing my hair which she described as a thick mop. Suddenly I felt so weak and bereft of the girl I thought I had become that I began to weep. They comforted me and told me that I wasn't to worry because

I was on the mend and I would be my old self again in a few days. Little did she realise how little I wanted to be my old self. One of the women disappeared, whilst the other rinsed my hair and asked me if I wanted to be soaped. I was beyond doing anything for myself so she started with a sponge and soap which smelled of roses as I lay back in the water. 'You have a wonderful figure,' she told me. She was the very first person ever to remark on my body, but then, she was the first person to see me naked since I had ceased being a little girl. She washed me with great thoroughness and then rinsed all the soap off, leaving only the scent behind. She instructed me to put my hands on the edges of the bath and to push as she lifted me. This wasn't as difficult as I thought it was going to be and I very soon found myself sitting on the edge of the bath. She had moved a cork-covered box, the same height as the bath, close to the edge. Her friend returned and together they got me out of the bath and began to apply warm soft towels to my skin. With a bit of assistance I was able to stand up and whilst one held me firmly the other dried me and rubbed moisturising cream into my skin. They put me into a towelling dressing gown and took me back to the bedroom. There I was surprised to see that the bed had been completely changed and that there were flowers in a vase on the window sill and some warm croissants and a hot drink on the bedside table.

Very shortly I was back in bed in clean pyjamas and feeling very much better than I had when I awoke. I must have sunk into a doze because I was awakened by my mother bringing me a tray with broth and toast on it and a hot drink. There were also three pills, which she told me that I had to take. 'You have had a very bad time,' she told me, but you are on the mend now.'

I slowly got through the food and took the pills with

the drink. I sank back against the pillows and stared at the ceiling. I began to recall events before I fell ill; my school; my success in the exams; getting to University in London, which I was due to start in October; my friends who were off on their summer holidays; my singularly dowdy wardrobe, filled with loose jeans and baggy tops, with the odd twin set and low-heeled shoes. I've no idea what set me off on those thoughts, but I recalled the restrictions on my social life and my parents telling me that it was far too early to be considering boy friends. Suddenly, like a bolt of lightning, I began to remember the scenes in my dreams. With my eyes closed I could call them all up.

I have long curly dark hair everywhere where you might expect to find long curly dark hair. The girl who was me was utterly different, except that she was, she was....I couldn't think what she was, except that all her experiences were not only ones I hadn't had, but also, until last night, I hadn't thought of. I've heard of life altering religious experiences, perhaps these were life-altering experiences of another sort. I lay in the warm bed thinking of what I had seen and partly shared and a warm shiver seemed to run through my body from somewhere between my legs. Surreptitiously I pulled at the elastic waistband of my pyjamas and slid my right hand down my belly. I encountered the fine bush that was well-termed my pussy. I gently opened the lips of my sex and slid my first and middle fingers between them. I had read about the clitoris in human biology books, but had dismissed the idea that this tiny lump of flesh had the sole function of providing sexual pleasure. Here I was, going on nineteen, and with no sexual experience. I concentrated on the succession of scenes I had been present at and on the gentle massage of my clitoris. I really must have been more deft than I gave

47

myself credit for. Within a couple of minutes I had begun to clutch my breasts under my pyjama jacket and tweak my nipples as the warmth in my pussy began to give way to a fluttering in my belly. I realised that it was all going to be over too soon, and also that it might just prove a little sticky. I had the strength of mind to stop for a moment and wad some tissues between my thighs.

I wondered if I had gone completely off the boil, but after a minute I knew that I was able to return to the earlier delights. I began to pant and I clawed my breasts unmercifully as I remembered the woodsman and then the couple in the loft apartment. I imagined that I was strung up as she had been and was being whipped, naked, before an appreciative audience. I felt the muscles in my belly contract and the fluttering become a powerful beat as the sensations moved up from my pussy, through my belly and into my chest, making my head swim and my breathing become laborious. I tortured my breasts and pressed harder and faster against my clitoris. I knew I needed something inside me, but that would have to wait the outcome of the pleasure I was giving myself.

I opened my eyes but my sight was blurred and I lost the image of the girl being laid on her back on the bed, and then, as I again watched her being whipped across her breasts, *my* breasts, I felt the delight of a sudden release. My head filled with pressure, the image before my eyes seemed to be subject to a zooming close up and I heard myself utter a muted version of her howl. Juice spurted from my pussy and I was taken over completely by the irresistible climax.

This was the first orgasm I had ever had, but I was determined that there would be many more. I wondered how long I would have to wait before it was possible to enjoy the whole process again. Meanwhile, I idly stroked my pussy and pulled at the hair which covered it. At once my mind was filled with an image of the blonde girl's pretty pussy and I began to wish that I had had my fur pruned and my hair cut, shaped and dyed. I wondered what my parents' reaction to that might be. As I began to drift off to sleep, quietly pleasuring myself, I had an image of the blonde girl in a skirt slit to the hip and a blouse undone to the waist. I saw her delicious breasts barely covered by thin material and fully exposed on their inner edges. I gave a great sigh. I wanted to be the blonde girl.

Over the next few days I stayed in bed with occasional forays into an armchair and the bath. I was undoubtedly gaining in strength, but my mind was taken up with the possibilities which had been revealed to me by my alter ego. I quickly learned that I could use my own fingers to give myself pleasure and that one orgasm could be soon followed by another. I was fearful of marking my skin in my enthusiasm, but even the doctor did no more than listen to my breathing in a most decorous manner and pronounce happily on my road to recovery.

After about a week, Louise, one of my friends from school, came to visit me. She has red hair and green eyes and is slender but curvaceous. I wished I looked half as beautiful as she did, and told her so. She was another whose appearance didn't please her, though I reckon she was in a minority of one. She told me she wished she had been a blue-eyed blonde. I began to tell her a slightly humorous and very much edited version of the scenes I had enjoyed. She was impressed even by the little I told her. She looked at me very hard and asked me if I was still a virgin. I blushed and said that I was, at least technically. We discussed men, university, freedom and sex. It was obvious to me that she was a great deal more experienced than I was, but I was discreet about my feelings concerning being displayed and whipped.

After half an hour she made her excuses and departed, kissing me, very agreeably, on the lips and saying that she would be back the following day.

I spent the earlier part of the night thinking about the scenes. It occurred to me that I could fall into almost any of them very happily, though I would try to avoid the backwoodsman. The following day Louise returned and produced a woman's magazine. Early on there were pictures of before and after with some rather unattractive women who had been subjected to makeovers. 'Think what they could do for us with such better material to work on!' I couldn't believe that she would want a change, but she sat on the bed close to me and we laughed at the fashion pictures. Louise was wearing a jersey print skirt and a blouse. It seemed very formal to me as I was used to seeing her in skin tight jeans and a T-shirt. There was a picture of a famous super model who was similarly dressed, except that her blouse seemed devoid of buttons and was open to the waist. I commented that it would be ideal for visits to the shops or the library. Louise commented that she could get away with it because she had virtually no boobs. I laughed and asked what happened if she quickly turned sideways. 'Nothing to fall out,' was the answer. 'Look, I'll show you.' Louise undid the buttons down the front of her blouse pulling it apart at the top and revealing a beautiful cleavage. She turned abruptly and a beautiful, firm, breast made its appearance. I was delighted and involuntarily reached out and held it in my palm. Louise looked at me and said, 'Go on, then.' I squeezed her breast and then took her nipple between my thumb and forefinger, rolling it and tweaking it. 'That's nice, try your lips.' I was astounded with myself that none of this seemed shocking or distasteful. In fact it was the very reverse. I nuzzled at her breasts and felt the nipples become turgid and a

50

little sticky. She kissed me and then reached into the pocket of her skirt. The next thing I knew, apart from the pleasure of licking her beautiful breasts was an unexpected vibration against my left breast. It made me draw in my breath and move my head back. Louise asked me if I liked the sensation. It hadn't gone on long enough for me to know that it was anything but surprising. She undid my pyjama jacket buttons and revealed my breasts. She made appreciative noises and applied the vibrating thing to my right breast. The sensation made me gasp and I cupped her breasts in my palms and pressed and pulled them.

'That's not where it's supposed to go,' she told me and before I had a chance to ask the obvious question, she had slid her hand and the vibrator down inside my pyjama trousers. She stood up and pulled my leg towards her and the vibrator touched my pussy. I looked at her with a mixture of horror and delight as she turned it so that it penetrated me and part of it caught against my clitoris. I lifted my hands to her head and pulled her face down to mine whilst the buzz spread its magic between my thighs. I kissed her and found my kisses returned with her mouth open and her tongue exploring mine and my mouth. Her free hand was on my breast as I slipped my left hand against her breast and fondled it. I was on fire with desire and excitement. She took her hand from my breast and lifted her skirt, revealing shapely white thighs topped by a dark golden crown of neatly pruned fleece. I did not need to be told that we should share our pleasure and I inserted two fingers into her pussy and pressed on where I thought her clitoris might be with my thumb. Her reaction was instantaneous and very pleasing, she kissed me again as my attention was divided between my own impending climax and making sure that she had the maximum pleasure. Very quickly my juices began to flow and she withdrew the vibrator and gave it to me. In a moment I had it inserted in her pussy and as my eyes closed with my own orgasm, prolonged by the use of my left hand, I thrust and twisted the tool so that it stimulated every part of her. Suddenly she threw up her hands and gave a small cry. I felt the juice running from her down the vibrator and into the palm of my hand. She bent forward over me and kissed me again.

Coming down from this experience was less than easy. She asked me if I was disgusted with her and I told her that I loved her and that I had done before this afternoon and now even more. I conjured an image of the scene I had enjoyed with the blonde girl and hoped that a longer and more intimate opportunity would present itself. We buttoned our clothes as my mother knocked on the door and entered with cups of tea. She warned Louise not to over tire me and Louise assured her that she would do nothing that might do anything of the sort. She and I smiled secretively and conspiratorially at one another. Louise drank her tea, kissed me again and fumbled in her shoulder bag. She had brought me a present, and some extra batteries.

The following day I had a visit from my uncle Richard. Uncle had enjoyed a happy, but not necessarily gay, bachelor existence whilst he made what were reputed to be very large sums of money buying and selling commodities. He always seemed to be able to work out just when something essential was going to be in short supply and buy as much as he could, selling it on as soon as the price had gone up to his satisfaction. I liked uncle Richard. He had a great sense of humour and would laugh uproariously at quite small things. He was utterly unlike my parents who were quiet and withdrawn and smiled from time to time but almost never laughed out loud. We went through the usual preliminaries and then he sat on the bed and looked earnestly at me. 'You could be anything you wanted,' he said. 'But you are seriously lacking in experience and you are constrained by the expectations of two people who I love very much, but who really need to let go of you. I am all too well aware that going to university is a very expensive process. As your Godfather I want you to be able to have the independence to do whatever it is you feel like doing. I have agreed with your parents that I shall finance you through university. Of course the Revenue and Customs tell me that I can only give you £300 a year without tax penalties. However, I am serious about this so I have opened a joint bank account in our names. You will receive the monthly statements and I shall only be involved if there needs to be a top up. My friendly bank manager will tell me and I shan't complain, provided you are enjoying yourself.'

I know I should have said 'Thank you,' but somehow that seemed very trite so I threw my arms round his neck and kissed him, several times. Eventually I ran out of breath and he sat back and laughed until the tears ran down his face. I felt a bit embarrassed and said 'Thank you uncle Richard.' But he just laughed a great deal more, until, caught up in the infection of his amusement and laughter I laughed in my turn. 'Hooray,' he said, 'I don't think you have reason to laugh enough. With a bit of luck that will soon change. In any case you must be getting better.'

'Uncle,' I said rather diffidently, 'would you mind if I used some of the money having a change of image?'

'It's yours to spend. What did you have in mind?'

I told him at some length. 'So she had all sorts of experiences you've not had and you think it would help to look like her. Why not, you'll still be my darling niece, and experience never hurt anyone.'

Just for once I suspected that he was not quite right in his estimation of the situation, though once again mine had been a very edited version.

It was a week before I was due to go off to London. I was fully recovered and went for a walk with Louise. We came upon the remains of Granger's farm. The fields had been bought out by a combine that owned a large amount of adjacent land. The burnt homestead was just as the fire had left it, but the nearby barn was untouched. We looked in at the doors. The season's hay crop was piled high in the barn. We sat on a large bale and swung our legs. Louise kissed me. I responded happily. She slipped her hand inside my coat and grasped my breast. It was defended by a thick jumper and a sensible bra. I put my hand between her thighs, but encountered sturdy denim jeans beneath the plaid coat she was wearing. It was chilly. We decided that eroticism was much helped by a warm environment, few clothes, or better, none at all, and a good deal of guaranteed privacy. We drew apart and laughed. I told her that I had arranged to go to a 'health farm' for my makeover. She asked me if I was going to become my alter ego and I realised that this was exactly what I had in mind.

The following day I left home on my own for the first time. I had explained to my parents what I was going to do, but not why, except that I liked the idea of a change of image. Daddy looked slightly surprised, but said nothing. Mummy started to voice her concerns, but now I was an independent person she saw the futility of her complaint and her monologue tailed off. The farm had an exotic name and offered so many options that it was difficult for me to make up my mind. I had brought a drawing of what I hoped my hair would be like and within an hour my unruly curls were being swept up. The bleaching process took rather longer but when the towel was removed and I saw myself in the mirror I gasped. I had my eyebrows thinned and then went to the depilation room. I was warned that electrolysis was rather uncomfortable and the effect was permanent. The two women started on my armpits as I lay on the treatment table with my hands under my head. They were right about the 'uncomfortable'. Each follicle was destroyed by a needle-like electric current. The day wore on, it became evening and I was tired and hungry. This part of the job was half done. As the older of the two women called a halt the younger moved suddenly and her probe accidentally touched the tip of my nipple. I was startled and slightly pained but my nipple reacted like a slut and stood out from my breast longer and harder than I had ever known it. It was tenderised by the current and as I slipped on my clothes I felt it respond to the touch of the cloth.

That night I lay in bed and made very good use of my vibrator. I imagined that the following day's attentions might make my pussy far too sensitive for any pleasure to be gained.

The following morning, after a careful bath and douche I was again taken to the

depilation room, but on this occasion there were three women with needles on the end of electric cables. Two continued as before, but the third produced an implement which I had not seen before, a battery driven clipper. She invited me to open my legs and I blushed as she piled the concealing towel on to my waist. I felt the buzz of the clippers as she ran them up and down my vulva. I knew that she was shortening my pubic hair and the buzz really wasn't at all unpleasant. She gently squeezed my outer lips and I felt the blades of the clipper close to penetrating me. A mix of fright and the insistent vibrating

55

buzz of the clippers began to make me feel the beginnings of arousal. How easy that had become, though I needed to concentrate on the more savage moments in my sleeping scenes to get the best result.

Fortunately the clippers had done their work. A big soft brush was stroking me and getting rid of the cut hair. I wanted to look at the result, but it was impossible because of the work going on under my arms. I had become used to the sharp pricks of the needles at my armpits, but the first sharp penetration of my pubic hair had me gasping. No, I didn't want an analgesic. I knew that I would soon adjust. With a break for coffee, work proceeded. My armpits were soon done and then there was the sensation of two operators working between my legs. The first woman explained that the pubic hair was coarser than the underarm hair and that there were fewer hairs per square centimetre. There would be fewer electric spikes, but each would be at a higher voltage to ensure the effectiveness of the treatment. I lay back on the treatment table and stared up at the ceiling. The fingers and probes at my pussy were unsettling. I wondered if I was different from other women as it was not as nice down there as I had hoped.

After a while I voiced my fears. I needn't have worried and was very reassured by the older woman's comment that I had as pretty a cunt as she had seen. There was a new word for me to use. I thought it was a term which passed the lips only of men. I was getting quite used to being wrong about a number of things.

The younger woman asked me if I had enjoyed the clippers. I blushed and looked away from her. She told me that a good half of the women who had a Brazilian asked for the clippers to be pressed against their vulvas so that they could have an orgasm. I realised that I had missed out unnecessarily. The really interesting ones were those who came when their labia were being attended to. Operators had been known to 'accidentally' touch a clitoris with the electric probe and watch the convulsions and gasping that followed. I supposed that they were not going to do this to me or they wouldn't have told me. It was about half an hour to lunch when I was asked to shift my legs, which I did. Fingers held my cunt and one seemed to have slipped inside me. I felt the touch of the surgical gloved finger on my clitoris and could not resist the temptation to press my buttocks upwards. This bit of unexpectedly wanton behaviour was rewarded by the biting touch of the probe against my clit and my response was an initial shriek and then a protracted moan as I felt all the muscles in my vagina contract and then open and a tremor set in as if all the parts of my pussy were flapping against one another. I twisted my body on the treatment table and let out a series of low cries and grunts until I became aware that my belly was going into repeated spasm, which was travelling up my body. I could not resist clutching my breasts and pulling at my nipples one of which still felt tender and excitable. In a matter of thirty seconds my ears were roaring and I was spilling juice onto the towelling cover of the treatment table. There was some laughter and then the clapping of hands in response to my reaction. Looking back I realise that this was a turning point for me - something I could never have imagined - a pain-induced orgasm in front of an audience.

I was ready to leave the Health Farm and stood naked in my bathroom in front of the long mirror. I didn't know what to think, but I was the image of the girl I had seen as me. I was amazed to think that with a minimum of makeup my mouth looked fuller and my eyes were subtly changed. My hair was exactly like the girl's. I had been warned to top up the colour at least once a week and to have it trimmed fortnightly. I looked at my breasts which were altogether larger than I had expected, and my waist which was narrower. It was my cunt that surprised me. There was not a hair in sight and the lips, which had been concealed since I started my periods, now showed as a neat, furled line extending further than I had imagined. I wanted to see if I could bring my clitoris to light and I reached down to pull my lips apart. There it was, a small bud of great pleasure. I touched it and the response was almost immediate. I would have to be very careful in the future. I wondered how it was that a woman can't tickle herself, but can use the same fingers to bring about a vast pleasure like an orgasm.

My next appointment was at a body piercing studio. If I had found the health farm difficult, I wondered how I would cope with quite such intimate contact as I had in mind. I soon found out. The studio was immaculately clean and polished. The receptionist confirmed the exact nature of what I wanted. She then warned me that all the tattooers and piercers were men, but that I could have her to chaperone me. I asked to be introduced to the man who was to do my piercing. He was a perfectly beautiful young man, but when I met him I guessed that his sexual preference was for his own kind and that I would be perfectly safe if he was competent. I refused the chaperone service and went with the delightful Gary to a curtained cubicle. He explained that the entire procedure would be recorded via CCTV, but that the angle of the camera was guaranteed not to show my face so that I would be unrecognisable, though the date and time were recorded throughout. He told me that the aim was to provide an electronic chaperone.

He described exactly what he was going to do and showed me the gold ornaments that he was going to use. I shivered a bit but he was quite matter of fact and as he pulled on his surgical gloves I removed my thong, lay back on the padded treatment table and waited. He pulled up my skirt, asked me to open my legs so that they dangled on either of the table and squirted my cunt with a spray of surgical disinfectant. He unfurled my lips and squirted inside them. He pressed my left lip with his finger and thumb and asked if that was the right place. I told him a bit further back. He found the place I wanted and told me that I shouldn't get fat or the bar would chafe my thighs. As I was in the middle of telling him that getting fat was the last thing I wanted to do I suddenly felt a startling pain which was so intense that I was, for a moment, unable to locate its exact source. I knew I had been pierced and that Gary was inserting the gold bar. I felt him twist the metal through the incision he had made. The ring supporting the bar was quickly and ruthlessly swivelled round and he used a beautiful pair of pliers to connect the ends.

As he stepped back I found that I was shaking. I saw that there was blood on his gloves. He insisted that I should see what he had done and produced a mirror for me to see the exact placing of the ring and bar. I took a deep breath and approved what he had done. At once he managed to replace the mirror and without any hesitation I felt the sharp sting of the second piercing. The process was repeated again and he invited me to get off the table and see myself in a full length mirror. I was very impressed by the neatness of his work, though the sting continued.

Gary explained that the clit ring was quite a different matter and was I sure that I wanted it done. I asked him if it would interfere with the sensations that could be generated by the clitoris and he assured me that if there was any effect it would be to heighten, rather than reduce my access to pleasure. I lay back again and the sting beginning to recede from my pierced labia. Gary told me that a clit ring could not be a matter of nearly, but not quite, and that it would be necessary for my clit to be much in evidence before it could be pierced. I thought it would be best if he did whatever was necessary. He handed me a folded handkerchief to put in my mouth and opened the upper part of my labia with his right hand fingers. He then inserted two fingers and began an up and down motion. I had done this to myself on many occasions after having learned from Louise. When I played this game I also had to imagine myself in my new guise as I had seen in the scenes in the huge hall. With Gary in charge I just lay back and enjoyed it. I felt a tiny flutter in my vagina and I could feel that my breathing had become faster and shallower. My little nub was becoming erect and slipping from its concealing sheath. I began to gasp, hoping that this would go on until I was able to spurt and scream and writhe. I felt Gary seize my clit between his thumb and forefinger and pull. This should have made me uninterested and even hostile, but instead it made me want to give myself to this handsome, but uninterested man. He squeezed and rubbed my clit between his finger and thumb until I could think of nothing except the desire for a climactic release. Suddenly my clit was struck by a pain of wholly enveloping proportions. I realised that he had pierced my erect clit and that he was still holding it away from the surrounding tissue. I couldn't get my breath to howl and as long as his fingers were in control of my clit I didn't want to move in any way which would cause me further pain. The ring was inserted and closed. He turned it in its piercing and I let out a low howl. He gave it a long pull and I gripped my fists beside the table to prevent myself from beating him. Eventually he seemed satisfied and let go of the ring. He put his arm under my shoulders and lifted me off the table. My legs wouldn't do what I wanted and I needed his support to make the short distance across the floor to the mirror. He insisted that I should inspect his handiwork. I pulled back my labia and there glinted my golden ring. I wondered just how much fun I might have with that in the future.

London was all that I had hoped it would be. I managed to find a studio flat and settled into the coursework and slight relationships with my fellow students without much difficulty. I wrote to my parents each Sunday and phoned Uncle Richard irregularly but frequently. I sent him a photo of myself and his reply was wholly approving. He wasn't the only one since I seemed to attract attention from men of all ages. I couldn't quite see why. In many ways I thought that my previous tousled black hair and informal clothes were more sexy than my current rather austere appearance. Perhaps they could use their instincts to look below the surface.

I went round to see one of my new friends, Emily. She lived in a very comfortable flat with Lisa. Emily was rather nondescript in appearance until she made an effort when going out or entertaining a boy friend. Then she scrubbed up most wonderfully, accentuating her brilliant bone structure by the addition of make-up expertly applied and revealing a slender but pretty sensational figure in dresses designed to show off her opulent cleavage and long, elegant legs. Emily knew exactly what her assets were and was happy to display them. On this evening she was her quiet self, which surprised me as she had a male visitor who was a very good-looking young man in his early twenties wearing wonderfully tight jeans and a cotton jumper advertising an international construction company. I introduced myself and found that I was talking to Emily's brother, Steven.

I knew I had to be careful to balance my attention between sister and brother. I would get nowhere with Steven if all I managed to do was to ignore and annoy Emily. Besides, I liked Emily and there was no reason why I shouldn't ingratiate myself with both of them. We talked of this and that and I asked Steven what he did. He told me he was in the building trade. Somehow I thought he might look just a bit out of place on a building site, but I held my tongue on that subject and asked what he built. He pointed out of the window at a building which dominated the landscape and told me that that was one of theirs. Emily laughed and pointed to his sweat shirt and told me 'that's us.' I still didn't get the point until she said, 'Think of my surname.' At that moment I felt very silly and extremely impressed. I apologised for not making the connection and blushed. Steven seemed to want to relieve my embarrassment and asked me what I was doing the next weekend. I thought of the course work I had to do but invited him to continue. After a slightly circuitous conversation he invited me to 'his place' for the weekend. Both Emily and Lisa would be coming and I could travel down in Emily's car.

Steven departed and Emily told me that I must have made a very good impression on Steven as it was unheard of for him to invite a girl to his home without knowing her very well first. She told me that she thought I would enjoy it because he lived in the country and there would be all sorts of games and amusements. I asked what these might be but was told to bring several pairs of jeans and skirts and shoes.

The drive seemed longer than I had expected, though I had no idea where we were going, so my expectations were irrelevant. We came to some high iron gates and Emily rummaged in the glove compartment for a remote to open them. They swung back to reveal a sharply curving drive, lined with huge mounds of rhododendron. Eventually the drive straightened and we were travelling through park land with some big trees and patches of saplings and bushes. There were occasional small buildings which I took to be summerhouses and then Emily swung the car to the left and I saw in front of me a large house with a vast gravelled courtyard in front of it. We had arrived.

Dinner was to be in forty minutes. I asked Emily what the dress code was. A dress or a skirt with a blouse, preferably with a couple of missing buttons. She smiled at me and took me to a room on the first floor. Her room was next door and beyond hers was Lisa's. She told me she'd knock on my door in half an hour. I unpacked and went into the en-suite bathroom which had everything that I could want. I decided on a shower. This short hair was very easy to manage and I was soon sitting in front of the big dressing table with its lights switched on and applying makeup. I decided on a dress which I had recently bought, hoping that it would be in keeping with the tastes and customs of my host. I held it up to the light and admired its crimson base overlaid with thousands of sewn-on beads. It was a short-sleeved cheongsam, tightly fitting but not quite in the Chinese tradition as it had a slit in both sides of the rather short skirt. I had time to change my mind so I put on a pair of fishnet tights and stepped into the sheath. I could just reach the zip at the back and drew it up, tucking myself neatly into the dress as it closed round me. I put on some ten centimetre heel court shoes and opened the wardrobe door so that I could see the full length effect. I was surprised and delighted, but also slightly apprehensive. My breasts were held in place by the dress itself, but I was sure that I could see every curve. It was a perfect fit round my waist and so well-draped over my hips that I saw that because of the angle of my pelvis in the high heels there was a hint of the mound at the top of my thighs. The side splits were essential for walking comfortably, but they made my legs look even longer than they were. I feared my bum

would look very large, but opening the other door of the wardrobe helped me to monitor my back view. I might have been biased, but I was pleased with what I saw. The only trouble was that I had no idea what other women would be wearing. I was about to take it off and try a skirt and blouse when there was a knock at the door. Surely I hadn't been half an hour.

I opened the door and found Steven in the corridor, dressed in a black suit and shirt and looking even more handsome than when I had seen him earlier in the week. He told me that he had come to apologise for not greeting me on my arrival. He put his arms round me and kissed me. He stepped back and looked me up and down. I asked if I was suitably dressed for dinner. 'Darling,' he replied, 'I wish you were the main course.' He was about to say more but Emily arrived towing Lisa with her. Lisa looked at Steven as if he was a God come to earth hopefully to ravish her, and then she took me in and her expression changed. Both Emily and Lisa were dressed in variations of the same theme. If I was displaying a wanton length of leg, they were revealing a substantial amount of cleavage. This was very tastefully and securely done in Emily's case, but Lisa looked as if she had been disturbed in the midst of trying to fix the open top of her dress and that it was sufficiently loose for even the casual observer to see not only the swell of her breasts, but as she moved the darker pink of her areolae, almost to the point of displaying her nipples. Any rapid movement in that dress would result in considerable fall out.

We were a very 'interesting' group as we descended

the staircase. Steven led the way followed by Emily, Lisa and myself. I had already worked out that walking downstairs in a dress as short and revealing as mine would give those on the floor below a lengthy view of my legs. At first I was rather shy about the impression that I might give, but I very soon changed my mind and remembered the old expression 'if you've got it, flaunt it', something which I had never done before. The people having drinks on the lower floor were a very mixed bunch in terms of age, attractiveness and dress. I was attracted to an older man who stood slightly apart, and having acquired a drink I left Steven to circulate among his guests, whilst I approached this unknown man who seemed surprised but delighted that I should select him to speak to. He was of middle height with a beard and moustache. His eyes hid behind glasses, but I noticed most of all that his hands were quite callused. We introduced ourselves. He was Charles and despite the evidence of his hands he told me that he was a writer. He also told me that he was present with Steven's permission to get a feel for the atmosphere and gain first hand experience of the events of the weekend. I asked him what these might be, but he appeared to be as uninformed as I was. Like all the men he was dressed in a black shirt and narrow black jeans. We began to discuss our fellow guests and I was able to look at them more closely. There was a tall blonde woman with her hair up, partnered by a man both older and more rotund than she was. She was wearing a satin dress which was well scooped out at front and back, to the extent that probably fifteen centimetres of cleavage was on view. She was heavily made up and was looking round the room at the other guests in much the same way as we were.

A woman in her early thirties, we guessed, with auburn hair and startling green eyes and an unbelievably curvaceous figure clutched the arm of a rather younger, blond man who bent his head to take in what she had to say. They were talking to a couple of young men who I immediately thought were gay, but I changed my mind when I realised that they were there to make up the balance of numbers. Finally, there was a girl who looked to be younger than me, dressed in a sort of shift which totally concealed her figure. She had fair hair in curls all round her head and hanging in her eyes so that she had to brush them away. She was talking to Lisa and Emily. There was the sound of a gong and Steven led the way to the dining room where we were able to help ourselves from a magnificent buffet. Emily sat on one side of me and Charles on the other. She warned me not to have too much as there would be dancing after the meal.

I like dancing, but this time it would have to be feet hardly moving, given the height of my heels, so upper body movement was the order of the day. I listened to the music which was being played as loudly as was possible without breaking the glassware. It was good to swing my hips and twist from the waist to jiggle my breasts. As soon as I started on this I remembered that I had omitted my bra. I felt my breasts slide inside the decorated material with my nipples being gently scraped by the stitching which held the beads and sequins in place. I found the sensation very agreeable and redoubled my efforts to echo the music by increasing my movements. The room was dark apart from some candles on the sitting-out tables and a spotlight which made its way among the dancers.

The tall blonde was doing much the same as I was without her partner. As the spot caught her I saw that her dress was of some material that was almost transparent under the fierce light. Like me she had decided that underwear would spoil the lines of her dress.

I was able to see that her small round breasts had quite lengthy nipples, which were pressing against the satin of her dress. No one needed to be in any doubt about her reaction to the music and her movements. She was soon joined by one of the 'spare' men who matched her very well.

The auburn-haired woman was rocking on her heels and swinging her magnificent body in time to the beat. On close inspection she appeared to be wearing a jacket with many buttons, all of which were done up from the neck to the waist. Her skirt seemed to be wrapped round her a couple of times and flew up with only the slightest provocation. Emily had undone the clasp which held the edges of her dress together over her breasts and even more delicious cleavage was on view, though I suspected that double-sided tape was ensuring that she didn't reveal too much of her breasts. Then there was Lisa. Until that night I had no idea whether I liked Lisa or not. I decided she was not my type. She was standing on the floor with her head well back and her eyes closed, hardly moving to the music. I decided that she had consumed a great deal too much alcohol and better be careful. I was amused to see that Steven had joined her, though until he touched her she was unaware of his presence. At once she became more animated and as the rhythm changed she started to give herself to the music. I had wondered earlier about the dress she was wearing and I watched in fascination as her breasts bounced and swung beneath the thin covering of material. I didn't have to wait long before they freed themselves from their covering and proved to be pert and nicely crowned with dusky pink areolae and prominent nipples. I expected her to be embarrassed and pull her dress over her pretty breasts, but instead she wafted them about with increasing abandon. The auburn-haired woman's partner had apparently undone her skirt at the waist and she was revolving so that after three turns he was left holding the skirt in his hand as she danced on in her jacket and a thong studded with brilliants. She had wonderfully curvaceous legs and a bottom of such padded magnificence that it seemed to invite caressing. Meanwhile, Emily had joined the blonde woman and they were dancing face to face. As Emily stepped back from her, the blonde's dress slid down her body. She stepped out of it to reveal the longest legs in the room, a scrap of material attached to threads to cover her between her thighs and a narrow waist and her delightful small breasts, pointed and with the nipples prominent. She continued dancing as if she was still fully dressed and received a ripple of clapping. Emily had turned to the girl in the shift and was encouraging her to dance. Once she started she was transformed and seemed to come alive in a way which couldn't have been predicted from her demure appearance. Emily had undone all the buttons of her blouse and her breasts were swinging with the rhythm. She danced close to the girl in the shift and stepped back with her blouse in her hand, still twirling her lengthy skirt. Lisa followed her example and Steven held her close to his chest in a rather unorthodox dancing hold. As they swung apart I saw that he had unhooked her skirt and she promptly became the second dancer reduced to a thong. I was surprised how well defined her figure was and also how she, like the blonde, kept dancing. Steven was obviously pleased with his handiwork, but was superseded as her partner by one of the spare men.

Steven elected to dance with me as we watched the auburn-haired woman whose partner hooked two fingers in her collar and gave a quick tug. Obviously the buttons were merely decorative and the jacket was closed with Velcro, and now no longer. She shrugged it off and he caught it as she revealed breasts of a magnificence to match her buttocks. For such a curvaceous woman it was a surprise that there was no surplus flesh, or the dimples which denoted a shifting fat layer. She brushed her partner's front with her magnificent breasts and continued to dance in her thong. Meanwhile, the girl in the shift had fallen into a sort of trance whilst following the music. The rhythm changed to jive and both she and her partner started to go through the elaborate steps until he grasped her and rolled her over his back. I had no idea how it was achieved, but she was wearing a dress at the beginning of the roll, but naked apart from a very small pair of white panties when she stood up on the other side of him. She seemed not the slightest bit concerned and they continued to dance together as if that had been the way of it since the beginning. I realised that I was the only woman still in her clothes. I didn't notice the two men who approached me from behind. I was unprepared for my arms being held and the hook and eye at the back of my collar being undone and the zip pulled down. In a trice my dress was pulled off each shoulder and then down over my hips. At the same time fingers were inserted into the waist band of my tights and these were tugged down below my knees. A third pair of hands slipped off my shoes and the tights were removed completely. I may have been the last woman to be stripped, but I had no covering at all. For a moment I felt embarrassed and slightly foolish, but I also got some applause and I slipped my shoes back on and continued to dance.

I wondered what all this was about, until the music stopped and Steven announced that it was time for some games. The first of these was the girls being jockeys to the men, and equipped with strips of canvas attached to a rod, each had to try to unseat as many others she could by belabouring them. I thought this was pretty bizarre but I was a guest and I thought I ought to co-operate. I chose Charles as my horse as he seemed to me to be solid and reliable and probably wouldn't let me fall off. I mounted his broad back and he gripped my thighs by slipping his forearms under them. I enjoyed the pressure of my cunt against his backbone and sought opportunities to grind myself against him. As the only naked woman I had chosen the oldest and most unthreatening of the men. Charles lined me up behind the girl in the white panties and I let her have a hefty strike across her back, followed by a slash to the buttocks. She was so surprised that she twisted too far in her mount's arms and they collapsed in a heap on the floor. Almost at once the blonde woman extended a long arm and her flail fell across my shoulders. I was surprised to be delighted by the pain and retaliated with a slash which went over her mount's bowed head and caught her across the breasts. She let out a cry and started to massage her breasts with her free hand. This was a tactical error as the auburn woman caught her two heavy slashes to her back and she managed to kick her mount behind the knee, bringing him down to his knees and then over on to his side as she mistakenly tried to hang on. I thought the redhead was going to have a go at me, but she moved away to where Emily and Lisa seemed to be battling it out. As they were intent on each other, her sudden attack, which I followed up, brought both of them sprawling. I was about to get in a heavy blow on the redhead's buttocks, but Steven stopped the game. He announced that we would face each other on the carpet, barefoot, and see who could win in one to one combat. I thought he meant that we would use the flails on each other, but he said we were to fight until one of us gave in.

The redhead was rather shorter than me, but she was

also heavier and looked decidedly strong. By this time I had forgotten that I was naked and the spirit of competition had taken me over. I was going to rely on speed and unexpected moves to win. We faced each other at a distance of a couple of metres. No scratching or biting, but otherwise all was fair. I watched my opponent's eyes as we circled one another, whilst the remainder of the group was sitting or standing around egging us on. I thought that at any moment she might launch herself at me and that I would have to move fast to avoid being knocked down. I made a few feints which caused her to close her arms over her chest, but I back pedalled away from her as fast as I could. She blinked and then, leaning forward as if to catch me, she threw herself at me. I was prepared for this manoeuvre and stepped to one side so that she grasped thin air. There was nothing to stop me from throwing myself onto her back, except that in passing her shin had caught my leg and twisted me round. I ended up lying across her back instead of parallel with it. Even so I thought I had a considerable advantage.

I caught her left arm and twisted it up her back, shifting my position so that my knees were on her thighs just below her buttocks. I tried the same grasp on her right arm, but was abruptly brought to realise that she was a great deal stronger than me. I could hold her arm with one hand round her wrist, but I could do nothing to effectively move her other arm with only one hand. I decided to ignore her free hand and smacked her buttocks with my unoccupied hand. This didn't seem to bother her so I leaned forward until my breasts were touching her back and started to insert my right arm under her neck, intending to get a lock on her and use it to stop her breathing. She seemed to have worked that tactic out and the next thing I knew she had rolled over, trapping

71

my right leg in the process and had wrenched her left arm from my grasp. I was lying with my left thigh between hers and my right leg under her. My only target now was her breasts and I seized one in each hand and started to pull and twist. They filled my hands and the sweat made them slippery. She had her left hand on my right breast and was matching my efforts. I knew I was being hurt but I had no other strategy than to keep up my attack. This was a mistake because I became aware that her right hand was between my thighs and that suddenly her fingers were in my cunt and her thumb penetrating my arse. I tried to escape her grip, but she seemed impervious to my attack on her breasts and moving my leg to kick her only allowed her greater penetration. Out of nowhere I suddenly felt a vice like grip between my cunt and my rectum. I prayed that she hadn't long finger nails, but she had me impaled. I left off my attack on her breasts and tried to lift the upper part of my torso so that I could get a firm grip on her wrist and remove her hand from between my thighs. I heard the sound of someone screaming with pain and realised that this was me. She was using her left hand to slap my breasts backwards and forwards so that they bounced and jumped under the contact with her palm and fingers. She had her fingers slightly clawed so that her nails raked my nipples each time she struck them. Her grip on my cunt became tighter. I saw the light of victory in her eyes, but I was not quite beaten. I dropped down onto her body and thrust my right forearm against her throat holding my right wrist with my left hand. She had only one arm to remove me. I closed my thighs on her hand and her fingers bit into my cunt with excruciating pressure. She started to cough and her face was suffused with a dark purple colour. I pressed harder and she squeezed more vehemently. I screamed. She

72

could not even gasp. Her eyes opened very wide and then closed, I felt her grip relax and I moved my forearm away from her throat. I felt her move her hand from its bitter grip and allowed her to twist her wrist. Almost at once I felt her fingers gently searching inside me and a pressure on my clitoris. She began to massage my clitoris with practised fingers and then her long middle finger struck my G spot. I gasped and put a hand either side of her head, dangling my breasts onto her face. She smiled and put her lips to my right breast, sucking in the nipple and holding it in her teeth. I was terrified that she would bite me, but instead her tongue curled round the tip of my breast and licked my nipple. I tried to reach down and pleasure her as she was me, but my position made it impossible. I was caught with my arse in the air, fingers in my cunt and my breast in her mouth. It wasn't so much that I couldn't move as that I didn't want to. I began to feel that strange buzz that becomes an urgent flutter in my belly and I realised that these clever fingers were bringing me to a climax. In the midst of her attentions I felt myself arch my back and tense my thighs and a voice cry out 'I'm coming' and I knew it was me and that the gushing release was my tribute to her victory. As the juices ran from me I bent my arms and lowered my face to hers and kissed her on the mouth. She smiled up at me and I longed to reverse our positions so that I could bring her the pleasure she had just given me. I became conscious of a sound around us and realised that I had forgotten that there were onlookers and that they were applauding.

Very slowly we unlinked our limbs and managed to stand up. I couldn't imagine why I didn't feel shame and embarrassment, but then there were five other very nearly naked women present, even though the men were still clothed. The redhead and I embraced long and warmly. I told her she was beautiful and wonderful and she replied that she hoped that we might meet again in not too different circumstances. Charles appeared at my elbow and the redhead's partner took her off to a table. Charles and I walked for a few paces and then heard the music of an old fashioned waltz. I wanted to be held close and made much of. He was sensitive enough to work out my wishes and we danced cheek to cheek, not easy with a waltz, but he never stepped on my feet. He asked me if I wanted to put on some clothes, but I saw that the women were still unclothed and that the men had removed their T-shirts. I tugged at his shirt and he got the idea and stripped off his jacket and the shirt underneath it. He was not a young man, but I was amazed by the solidity of his body and the clearly defined muscles in his arms and back. He explained that he lived in a wood and looked after the trees and that such an activity kept him fairly fit. I felt quite fragile held in his arms and pressed against his powerful chest. I began, for the first time, to realise what girls see in older men. At that moment I determined to see more of Charles.

I thought there would be more interesting activities that night, and I suppose that in a way there were, since couples got together. I noticed that Steven had decided that the girl who had been in the shift dress was much to his taste. For a moment I had a pang of jealousy, but I realised that I had concentrated on Charles and that Steven might be trying to tell me something.

Eventually, I told Charles that I ought to collect up my clothes and go to bed, after all, who knew what Steven's vivid imagination might think up for the following day? Charles escorted me to my room. I noticed that Emily and Lisa had already departed. As we walked along the corridor we heard sounds that made me think that neither of them was alone. Charles gallantly kissed my cheek at my door, but I clasped his hand and towed him into my room. He didn't seem to object.

Writers make much of the romantic encounter in the girl's bedroom. OK, I suppose the sex was nice, and it was, all three times, but I am not used to sharing my bed, even a sizeable double bed, and I found it difficult to sprawl out as I usually did without coming into contact with Charles who must have thought that I was insatiable. He did a very good job of being asleep and not snoring and lay on his face with one knee out of the bed.

In the morning I slipped out of bed and into my bathroom. When I returned, very much refreshed, I found that Charles had departed. At first I was a bit miffed, but I thought that he might just have been tactful. We greeted each other at breakfast and enjoyed the meal together. There were place cards on the table and each had an envelope as well. The letter inside was from Steven. Everyone was to assemble at the summer house by the swimming pool at ten o'clock. Dress was to be strictly informal. Charles was his usual charming self, but told me he had no idea what was then going to happen. He thought we might all have a splash in the pool, but somehow I doubted it.

Trainers, jeans and a T-shirt struck me as the most practical and informal clothes I had with me. Charles called for me at ten to ten and we made our way to the pool. Most people were already there, and the stragglers soon joined us. Emily asked me if I had enjoyed the previous evening as much as I appeared to. Unexpectedly I blushed, but my smile was the widest I could produce. I wondered if she knew just how many enjoyments I had had. Charles certainly had stamina to go with his strength.

Steven appeared and told us that this morning there would be a variety of amusing things to do. They were written down and contained in sealed envelopes. Each of us could take an envelope and then read what we were to do. He fanned the envelopes out in his hand. It seemed to be chance that determined our choice. I found that with Emily and the girl in the shift, I was to have a fishing lesson at the lakeside, shared with two of the spare men. Lisa, the redhead and the blonde were to go to the orangery and help with training the bushes and trees. It all seemed very tame to me, but at least it would be different. We made our way to the lake and encountered a tough-looking character who described himself as a water bailiff. He was to be our tutor. He taught us about rods and lines and bait and casting and despite myself and a not inconsiderable dislike of fish and an aversion to giving animals pain, I found it interesting. At last we had some practical exercises and we stood in a row on the river bank attempting to cast our lines over the lake. He told us to keep a firm grip on the rod and never to let it go. The girl who was dressed in another shift was the first to cast her line. I saw her neatly-tied 'fly' hover over the water. She was obviously possessed of skills I didn't think I had ever learned, and was going to ineptly demonstrate very soon.

I cast my line and overdid the throw so that the bait and hook and the end of the line disappeared into the weeds some ten metres away. I started to reel the line in, but it was fast in the weeds. Rather disconsolately I turned to our instructor and asked what I should do. He looked at me with a mixture of surprise and exasperation and told me to go into the water and release it. His tone didn't seem to brook any argument. He held my rod and I removed my trainers. I started down the bank when I heard him shout that I must take off my jeans as full of water they would be dangerous. I turned my back to him and undid the clip and opened the zip. When they were off I was aware that my abbreviated cotton panties covered very little of me. However, I was glad that I had taken his advice as I slid off the bank into the water. Oh! It was cold. Close to the bank it hardly covered my ankles, but it sloped down quite quickly. My first step brought the water almost to my knees. The second step allowed me to feel the chilling grasp of the water halfway up my thighs. I knew that the third step would begin to chill me significantly. I wasn't quite correct. At that point the bottom must have flattened out a bit and the third step, brought the water well up my thighs but only just touched me between them. I felt the icy fingers clutching at the thin material of my panties. For a few seconds I dared not go further, since I was imagining the water striking my belly. I plucked up my courage and began my fourth step. I felt the cold water rise up my thighs and seize my cunt in its chilling grip, it made me gasp. I felt unsteady and reached out to the end of a branch which was dipping in the water. I heard the waterman shout at me to get a move on. The water was now caressing my belly and filling my navel with an unfriendly finger. I held on to the end of the branch and stepped forward. My foot found nothing and I tried to retrieve my step, but my hold on the branch merely bent it down into the water. I let go and felt the twigs scrape up my back. I was trying to settle my feet on the firm bottom of the lake, but the branch caught in my T-shirt and held me still. I was fast losing my footing and beginning to panic. My attempt to get back on to the solid bottom was thwarted, my feet went from under me and the branch ripped my T-shirt and scored my skin. I found I was hanging on the branch by a broken bit of wood caught in the neck band of my torn T-shirt. It was doing its utmost to strangle me. I pulled the ripped garment over my head and landed in the deep running water, which closed over me. I struggled to gain a footing and found that the water was over my breasts. Moving from now on would be difficult and my position was precarious.

Fortunately, I could see the line glinting in the sun and the end of it was only a short distance away. I decided to plunge forward and this seemed to work well as I arrived at the hook end of the line. I heard our instructor telling me to be careful as I didn't want the hook in my fingers. I found the end of the line and the float and reached for the hook. This had caught in a submerged branch in the weeds and I very carefully unwound it and held on to it. I felt a sense of achievement and turned towards the bank with my prize held aloft. I saw that my T-shirt, or the remains of it, was caught in the branch I had held on to. The waterman began to reel in the line and I let go of the float. It was time to get back on dry land. I stepped forward, forgetting the hole into which I had fallen on the outward journey. In an instant I was wholly submerged. The current of the stream was washing over the whole of my body and I was thrashing about in an effort to regain the vertical. As I came to the surface and took a deep gasp of air I realised that the current had taken me several metres down stream from the tree and my T-shirt. There were new hazards which included a long root from one of the trees. I held on to this as the water tugged at my body. I felt it snatching at my one remaining garment and tried a desperate attempt to pull my panties up, but the water was too deep and they were already below my knees. In a moment they were on only my left ankle. I didn't want to regain the bank naked, particularly after the previous night when I had been the only naked girl there, and in any case I was a bit put off by the possible reaction of the waterman. I held on to the submerged root and drew myself along it, hand over hand until I approached the bank.

To my horror there was the waterman looking down at me. He put my jeans on the bank and then took off his jacket. I began to forget everything about my situation except that I was cold and miserable and naked and this oaf obviously had it in mind to take advantage of me as I stepped up the bank. I watched him as he drew off his jumper and then unwound from his waist a length of rope which he attached to the tree. So he was going to tie me up and then....

He left his jumper on top of my jeans, threw the rope expertly towards me. He told me to hang on to it and towed me to the side of the bank. I crouched in the chilling water awaiting my fate, but instead he asked me if I could get up the bank OK and invited me to put on his jumper once I had landed. He turned his back and began to walk away. I heard the sound of his voice talking to the other two girls. Girded into action I used the rope to scramble up the bank and for a few seconds danced on the grass to get my circulation going and to shake off as much of the water as I could. I slipped into my jeans and then picked up his jumper. I don't like other people's clothes, but as I began to put it over my head I breathed in a heady musky scent of new sweat and a body odour which must have been composed wholly of male pheromones. This man had far more about him than I could ever have guessed from looking at him as he supervised our efforts at fishing. As I approached the others I saw that he was just straightening up from taking a hook out of a trout's mouth and slipping the fish into a keep net. I realised that I was shivering uncontrollably, despite the warm day. He told me to put on my trainers and then took my hand in his big hard fingers. He called to me to come on and set off at a slow trot, at first hauling me along, but then, as I began to get my joints and muscles working I came alongside him. We had started

79

very slowly to give me a chance to be able to move without hurting myself, but after two or three minutes he increased the pace, still holding on to my wrist. To my utter amazement I found that I was enjoying the running and the close presence of the tough man. We went faster and I wondered if I could manage to out run him, come to that I was very surprised that he could move so swiftly and effortlessly. He gave the impression of strength, but strength that was exercised unhurriedly. I hadn't equated him with running. I realised that I was no longer cold and that I was beginning to sweat in the thick jumper. As we approached a small group of trees I told him that I thought the cure was complete. He didn't stop at once, but guided me between the trees. He told me that he had to be sure I enjoyed the fishing and getting frozen in the water wasn't a good way to do it. We stopped and he turned to me, still holding my hand. He looked very deep into my eyes and told me that it was many a long lonely year since he had held a beautiful young woman in his arms and kissed her and would I mind if....I didn't answer but wound my arms round his neck, pressed myself against him and kissed him for all I was worth. I heard the rapid intake of his breath as he hugged me to him and I felt the immediate pressure of his erection on my belly. I smelled the scents of his manhood filling my nostrils with desire. I wanted him to crush me against a tree and fuck me. Only the need to return to the others stopped me from unzipping him there and then. I whispered in his ear that at some time in the future he would receive a little reward for his kindness and helpfulness to me. He smiled, revealing an amazingly even set of white teeth and told me it might be more than he deserved.

We ran back to the others who were sitting on the bank sunbathing. He asked them if they had enjoyed their morning fishing and they all seemed to have done. The girl in the shift asked him what was to become of the fish they had caught. He looked at her quizzically and asked what it was she would like to do with them. She went a pale shade of pink and said that they should be returned to their lives as son as possible. He seemed delighted, looked for Emily's and the men's agreement and tipped the bottom of the net up and our captives swam away, apparently none the worse for what must have been a harrowing experience.

We made our way back to the house. Emily led the way with the pale girl, deep in conversation. I walked next to the water bailiff and asked him his name. He was George. I told him that I would return his jumper if he would tell me where he lived, which was the end mews flat. I told him that I would wash the jumper first. He said I should do nothing of the sort. He said he liked the scent of clean bodies and that what little I left for him would remind him of me when I was no longer there. I was quite overcome by this and told him that I would leave it outside the door as soon as I had changed, though I thought I would like to see him again if he was in after he'd finished work. I got the full benefit of another smile and we arranged to meet at five thirty.

I went to my room and took off the clothes I was wearing. I held his jumper up to my face and breathed in his essence. I hoped that he would still like me by the time we met in the afternoon. I showered and changed my clothes, putting the jumper between the pillows on my bed. It was lunch time and we all assembled for a drink. I told Charles an edited version of the fishing. He told me that he had been to see what the two groups of men were doing and had been hauled into going on to the roof and repairing the lead strips which secured the slates. He didn't think it was a skill that he'd ever use again, but it was interesting to see how the roof was constructed and how big it was. We were joined by the redhead, who looked invitingly at me and told us that they had been to the orangery where the temperature started at about twenty degrees Celsius and very quickly rose from there. She had been inducted into the art of pruning and thinning the grape vine, which she had enjoyed, though the heat meant that they all wilted a bit and walked through the greenhouse misting system in order to keep cool. This had led the head gardener to make a comment about Miss wet T-shirt and the blonde had flashed her boobs at him. This rather set the tone of the morning which ended with an invitation to Lisa to visit the propagation shed. I began to think that Lisa was a real little goer, until I blushed as I thought of myself.

We had lunch sitting round a vast circular table which could have accommodated even more than the dozen of us. I sat next to Charles on one side and Steven on the other. Steven asked me about the morning and I told him I had got very wet. He didn't pursue me for details but he asked me what I would like to do in the afternoon. I could have told him that I would like to share Charles or George's bed, but that's hardly the way to treat one's host, though come to think, I wouldn't have minded Steven's bed, either. He asked me if it would appeal to me to play a sort of charades, but where the participants took the parts of a famous painting and the rest had to guess what it was. He had a list of likely scenes and the 'dressing up box' would provide the costumes.

Steven suggested the idea to the others who seemed to be pleased to take part, though most of them were still slightly puzzled about the skills they had learned during the morning. Steven produced a handful of cards and told us that we would each have a choice and that we could call on others to assist us where there was more than one person needed. The lawn round by the south wing was to be the venue. Emily showed us where the dressing up wardrobe was kept, in a substantial room crammed with the discarded clothing of a very rich family, and some which had obviously been kept from theatrical performances. I selected costumes for my two helpers and my own, together with one or two small props. I was asked by Steven if I would be in his picture and agreed and I also agreed to help Charles. I did get a couple of other offers, but I thought that three were quite enough. Steven had put numbers on the cards and these indicated the running order. The very first was the appearance of four of the men carrying what looked like a chaise longue covered in a sheet. They placed it before us, drew off the sheet and joined the rest of us. They had exposed the nude body of the redhead with her ankles crossed and her hands behind her head and elbows out, reclining on several cushions. We stared in some surprise and then clapped when Charles called out: 'Goya, Maja Desnuda'. The redhead was delighted and having let us take in her voluptuous body, with which I was already very well acquainted, she laughed, reached down for the sheet and swung her legs off the cushions and returned to the house.

The next tableau made use of the fountain. The five of us remaining women, having removed our clothes, but holding tastefully-draped towels, assembled at the fountain and took up suitably languorous poses. We were guided by one of the spare men. There was a lengthy pause as the men gazed at us, perhaps daring one of them to break the spell. Eventually Charles said the single word: 'Ingres,' and we applauded him as the men applauded us. There was a gap here as we put on our clothes and the men dressed for their next scene. There were no naked figures in this tableau, which was Charles's. The pale girl, dressed in antique boy's clothing, was standing in front of a table with Charles leaning towards her with his finger pointing, whilst the other men stood about looking large in comparison with the girl's slight figure. We looked at one another but could make nothing of it, until the blonde suggested: 'When did you last see your father?' We were at a loss to name the painter so it was evens. The next tableau involved me, the redhead and Steven. I was naked apart from a thin veil of cloth draped from my shoulder to between my knees. Charles tied me to the fountain. The redhead entered wearing a strange animal suit and Steven entered wearing nothing, but carrying a sword and a shield. He took up his stance before the redhead and waited. We three knew that this was a complete pastiche and it wasn't surprising that the others looked rather diffident about suggesting a title. A little breeze disturbed my drapery and Steven shifted his position so that the others shouldn't see that he was giving signs of interest in my now naked body. At last someone suggested a title, but somehow it really didn't fit with the slaying of the Minotaur. It was agreed that we had won.

The blond man was next on the scene revealing a muscular, lightweight figure, quite naked and holding what looked like a dinner plate in his right hand. He bent forward and drew back his right hand. There was silence until Charles whispered into one of the men's ear 'Discus thrower' but of course that was a sculpture, so he was cheating.

We were definitely getting into the swing of things now. A divan was brought out and the pale girl lay on it, covering herself to the neck with the useful sheet. We could see that her left leg was dangling over the side of the divan. Almost at once one of the spare men appeared, quite naked and revealing a lengthy cock dangling between his thighs. He approached the girl, pulled off the sheet and held her with his hand round her throat. What had been dangling was now rampant and was very close to the faintly fleeced slit between her legs. She held his wrist with her hands as he clasped her breast with his free hand. No trouble there, The Rape of Lucrece. There was a cry to encourage the dark man to complete the tableau, but the pale girl promptly put her hands between her thighs and this tableau came to a slightly disappointing end.

The last of the four men appeared next complete with the blonde. He was dressed in the smallest of thongs designed more to make us wonder what would happen if he became interested in the woman beside him. He reached up, showing some well-defined muscles and an enviably flat belly and attached her wrists to one of the side sprays on the fountain so that her already tall figure was further elongated. He tore open the shapeless tunic which she was wearing and revealed her naked. Because we were all entranced by the slender, but toned, body of the nude we did not notice that he had picked up something from the ground. It was obviously a means of punishment, in fact a whip. He shook out the numerous tails and turned towards the blonde. Slowly he drew an arc with his arm and the tails struck her across the shoulders. She shook and uttered a little cry, but there was no further action. The man froze in the position which he had taken when his whip struck his partner. We looked at the very appealing tableau, but could not recall a painting which looked like this, unfortunately. 'We' didn't include Charles who muttered something which I only half heard. I turned to him and he repeated, 'The scourging of Ruth.' I volunteered the title and the dark man smiled. A voice urged on him to penetrate his victim, but she pointed at the open doorway to the house and they exited, probably with the intention of doing in private what they were not prepared to do in public.

This left only Emily and Lisa. I guessed that Lisa would be keen to show the assembled men what they were missing. At last, both of them appeared, wearing only skirts but balancing large earthenware pots on their heads which they held steady with one hand. I must say that I admired the appearance of strength and also the curves of their bodies down to their skirts which were held on one hip, the other side of the hem being well down towards their thighs. There was a good deal of muttered conversation among the onlookers, until Charles once again saved the day with a reference to Sir William Russell Flint. It had been a change from charades and had almost started to get interesting, particularly with the blonde and her partner. Before we had a chance to disperse Steven called us to order and produced another set of cards. Mine had instructions to go into the sitting room, remove my clothes and drape a sheet across my body. We trooped into the house and I was surprised that all of us seemed to be doing the same thing. Steven came round to each of us and put a blindfold on us. From what I could hear he was taking people back on to the lawn. Eventually he came to me, though I was not the last. I felt the grass under my feet as I held the concealing drape in front of me. He instructed me to kneel down and then left me. It was warm and pleasant and I waited to see what would happen next and where the others were. I hadn't long to wait. Steven instructed us to remove our blindfolds and I blinked in the bright sun to see all of us present with the women mostly lying on their backs or on one knee or both as in my case. Charles was immediately in front of me, insecurely draped, as I was, and tensed as if he was about to engage in some athletic contest. Steven had again chosen the pale girl and he called out 'Rape of the Sabine Women'. At once there was a good deal of movement, laughter and some protests. The men had all launched themselves at their partners. Charles drew me up from my kneeling position and inserted a knee between mine In a moment he had rendered us both naked and had bent me back from the knees, whilst he pushed himself between my thighs. I could feel the hot throbbing helmet of his cock touching my cunt, but he made no attempt to penetrate me. He bent forward still further and kissed my lips. He had a hand either side of me flat on the grass. It would have been the work of only a moment for him to push himself inside me, but instead he whispered in my ear that this was not the time or place and I reached up as far as I could and hugged him. Out of the corner of my eye I could see that the blonde and her partner were fully engaged as were the redhead and hers. Lisa was being tightly held by another of the men and Emily was lying on her back with her legs and arms apart, being slowly shafted by the dark man who had whipped the blonde. Steven was kneeling between the pale girl's open legs, but she had her hands on his cock and balls and was rubbing one and squeezing the others. There was obviously going to be no penetration there, or so I thought, except that Steven exhibited his substantial strength and flipped her over so that she was lying on her front. He held her down with a hand in the middle of her back whilst he thrust his fingers into her cunt and began to work on her as she squirmed under him. She made the mistake of trying to get her legs to bend at the knees, probably with the intention of pushing him off and running away. As she drew her knees up towards her chest, which was still firmly pressed into the grass, her buttocks rose, too. This must have been the very opportunity which Steven had been looking for and he thrust himself forward. All was not quite as either of them had intended and she found herself impaled in the darkest of places. She let out a cry of pain and despair, but once securely in her arse Steven was apparently not going to stop, and he didn't though she wailed and cried out.

It was difficult to imagine the motivation of the couples. The spare men seemed to have decided that they must act out their parts, come what may, Charles was behaving like the gentleman I knew him to be, though perhaps his care was just a little disappointing. Steven, on the other hand was intent on ravishing the so far impenetrable girl. That he had penetrated her arse rather than her cunt was almost hilarious, though I began to think that she just might have been a virgin in both. I knew what a shock this must have been to her as she lacked the preparation which I had enjoyed.

As if to save the Sabines from their cruel fate, a small puff of wind brought with it a shower of rain. Given my experience in the morning this didn't bother me at all, but the others, including Charles, started up, clutched their drapes and turned to the house. I felt the pattering of the warm rain on my skin and loved every moment of it. I was conscious that Charles was asking if I wanted him to stay, but I signalled that I was happy to stay on my own and he departed whilst I felt the sensuous trickles on my skin, running between my breasts, filling my navel and coursing down the valley between my hips and my belly to drain across the naked skin of my cunt. I found myself with my fingers between my legs. But before I could enjoy the entire sensation I saw one of the gardeners with a wheelbarrow a few metres away and I followed the others into the house.

Having regained my clothes and my room I looked at

my watch and realised that it was fast approaching five thirty. Having showered, and brushed my hair, I sought out a T-shirt and jeans, put on my trainers and gathering up the borrowed jumper I went down the main staircase and out of the front door and round to the back of the house where the stableyard was situated. I was early for my appointment, but the door was open and I gave a little cough and entered, closing the door behind me and slipping the bolt across. George came out of a room which branched off the entrance hall. His many layers of morning clothing had been replaced by a brief pair of boxers and a polo shirt. He welcomed me and asked if I would like a cup of tea. He held out his hand for the jumper, but I dropped it on a chair and caught hold of his wrist and drew myself against him. For a moment he seemed surprised. I thought he was sufficiently modest not to expect too much for himself. I liked that and was pleased that he did not try to rush me or take me for granted. He bent his leonine head and kissed me. I was not slow in returning the kiss. He had obviously just had a shower, but that delicious musk was returning. He asked me if the afternoon's games had been enjoyable. I said I thought that people hadn't got into the swing of things yet, but give them time. He laughed and complimented me on my ability to keep up with him when we ran in the morning. He explained that he spent a good deal of time keeping fit. He opened a door and showed me a room filled with what I took to be equipment from a high tech gym. As I looked I thought that there was something odd about all of it, but I couldn't put my finger on just what was wrong. He asked if I would like to try any of it, and despite my desire to have him as a lover I postponed the moment and he showed me the treadmill. This had a large readout which told the runner all that she wanted to know, and a good deal more besides. I thought it was a good idea, given how boring exercise of this sort can be. I stood on the endless belt and he wired my forearms to the support rail. He switched on the machine and the track began to move so I started to walk. At that moment there was a ring from the telephone and he excused himself. I realised that this was a very sharp piece of kit. I read my pulse rate, oxygen intake, speed of the track and numerous other details. What I hadn't realised was that it was interactive and was searching for the speed that gave the maximum of cardio and aerobic exercise. The speed started to increase and my feet moved faster, and faster and faster. Sweat was breaking out all over my body and was running out of my hair into my eyes. I called out, but there was no response from George. My T-shirt was soaked and clinging to me. I tried lifting myself on the support rail but the stretching did no more than make my jeans rather insecure. I was gasping when the door opened and George reappeared. He rushed in apologising profusely and cursed himself for leaving the mill on auto. I came to an abrupt sweaty halt. He started to unwind the cables that had held me. He asked me if I would like a shower but I said I'd like to get out of my sweaty clothes. This time he stood and watched as I dragged the wet T-shirt over my head and drew down the zip of my jeans and stepped out of them. He told me that he would put them in the dryer, and then that exercise was best undertaken naked. I had recovered from the encounter with the treadmill, but there were several other machines that looked more interesting. I've always admired athletes on parallel bars and rings. I thought I'd try the rings. I jumped up and grasped them and at once my wrists were held in thick leather bracelets. Just to stop you falling if your hands are sticky, he explained. I hung, naked, in front of him and he suggested a number of things I could do. I did them. They all seemed to me to give him an even better view of my body, not that I minded, because I could see the very evident interest he was showing, pulsating inside his boxers. I pushed my hands apart and opened my legs. It was hard work, and I felt rather like a victim. He reinforced my impression by asking if I had ever been whipped. I told him that I hadn't but that I'd seen one of the guests whipped that afternoon. He stood behind me and I found that his hands were reaching up to my breasts. He made various complimentary comments and cupped my breasts in his hands, tweaking my nipples. I felt a little twinge of warmth between my thighs. His hand slipped down to between my thighs and he inserted practised fingers in my cunt. I shook as he searched for my clitoris. He managed to keep his fingers working on me as he walked round to face me. He stood up tall and sucked my nipples, curling his tongue round each of them and then taking them in his teeth. He bent and at the same time removed his fingers from my cunt, only to use his thumbs to open my lips with his thumbs and sink his tongue between them. This at once made my clitoris come to life in a way which was quite new to me. The lapping of his tongue was in tune with the pulsing of my vagina. I wanted him to take me down from the rings and penetrate me, but I was so overcome with the passion of the moment that I could think of nothing but the pleasure that he was giving me. The pulsing turned to a distant thunder which roared through my body and filled my mind with the furnace of passion. I knew there was only one outcome and that very soon arrived as he stepped back and watched me kick and writhe and cry out as juices spurted from me and I was overtaken by the release I had sought. As it began to subside he told me to hang on and he released the cuffs by pulling a small tag on each of them. He held me under my buttocks and told me to let go. I uttered a cry as the pressure came off my arms and I fell forward, burying his face between my breasts. George was very strong. He carried me out of the gym and into a cool plain bedroom with a brass bedstead on the middle of one wall. He dropped me on my back on to the bed so that my bottom was on the edge and my feet and legs dangled towards the floor. I was surprised how high it was. I realised that he was pulling off his polo shirt and stepping out of his boxers.

They say that size doesn't matter, it depends on the man's expertise in using it. Sometimes there is a big one with an expert behind it. This was most certainly true of George. I lay back as he stood between my thighs and grasped my breasts. I felt him move his hips back, release one of his hands and guide his magnificent erection to the slightly open slit of my cunt. His cock touched me and it was like an electric shock. I stiffened for a moment as this monster pressed harder and harder into me, but oh, so slowly. I thought he was about half in when he started to withdraw with equal slowness. I don't know how often he pressed in and out again until the end of his cock struck the neck of my womb, but it seemed to go on for hours and I became dizzy with the pleasure of his pressure and withdrawal, the feeling of his cock sliding into me and then being slowly taken right out until its dripping head was again shoved against my tender tissues. Then I began to feel the strangest fluttering between my legs and the beating of wings in my belly, the motion of the internal pressure making me completely out of control as it moved up my body. There was an explosion in my head and as I called out with what little breath I had left, I encountered the dark demon of complete renunciation of self-control.

All the muscles of my body went into spasm, my belly

contorted and I gripped the invading prick as if it were the only lifebelt in a stormy sea. I could no longer see or hear or feel the world around me, everything was concentrated on the final plunge of his sword into my cunt. As it came I screamed and everything went dark. I was still conscious because I could feel great spurts of juice hitting his thighs and running down mine. And then there was a hoarse howl as he joined his jism to my juice and we were driven to what I thought was the ultimate in passion.

I awoke some time later to find myself covered by a light blanket and enfolded in his arms.

The evening meal was soon over and I waited to see what Steven might have to say. He awarded a prize to the blonde for her part in the tableau in the afternoon and hoped that we might all see more of her in the future. It looked to me that I was not the only one who had had some entertainment following the afternoon's game. Steven suggested that we might like a quiet evening and an early bed, because tomorrow there would be breakfast at six a.m. followed by a track event to decide the fastest of the men and women. This would be followed by a picnic and then a romp in the parkland. I was pleased to think I might quietly slope off to bed. I had engaged in a long day of activities and needed time to reflect. I lay back in the fresh sheets considering the day that had passed. Naked, chilled and soaking in the morning. In the afternoon, a spectator at a variety of scenes and a participant in more than one. I recalled my envy of the blonde woman. How I wished that this might have been me. The sex with George was utterly wonderful, but somehow I felt the need to be admired in public, and by as many people as possible. A little pain added in and I would achieve Nirvana. I drifted off to sleep thinking how this desirable situation might be achieved, but without any very firm solution.

We gathered on the lawn. I wore my accustomed T-shirt and trainers, plus a pair of shorts. Because I knew that we were to engage in races I had put on a solid sensible bra which almost held my breasts steady. The men had the first race and one of the spare men came an easy first. Charles trailed along behind the others. The blonde proved herself to be fitter than I am and a great deal faster. The pale girl had a good turn of speed, but the auburn-haired girl trailed the field. Emily and Lisa managed to be fourth and fifth to my third and the pale girl's unexpected second. For some reason I feel disappointed that I didn't do better, but I reflected that the first two are both light and not particularly curvaceous. It was still quite early and Steven suggested that we might bring forward the afternoon's proposed activity and have a go at hares and hounds. The girls could set off and be given a two minute advantage over the men. Their job would be to catch us and the man who caught the most was to be the winner. Any girl not caught in half an hour was to be the female winner. I considered that this would have little to do with speed so much as concealment. Not far from the house on the left hand side was a wood, once in there I thought that it ought to be possible to evade the hounds.

There's something about running away from those who wish to catch us which causes the heart to race and the glands to excrete all sorts of helpful hormones. I took off with the others, but lagged behind as soon as we had passed the concealing wall and turned away and made for the wood. I hadn't explored this before and was unprepared for the undergrowth, which had numerous barbs in it which caught the skin of my legs and tore at my clothes. By that time I was thoroughly psyched up and was determined not to be caught. I made the best way I could through the trees and brambles, avoiding the slashing bushes wherever I could. I looked over my shoulder but could see no one following me. I stood still and listened and caught the distant sound of a heavy body crashing through the undergrowth. I must now do something about concealment. I ran on as quietly as I could until I found myself in a glade carpeted in short grass with several very large trees sheltering it. One of these had branches touching the ground. I decided to climb it and see if I could hide in the foliage. The ascent was easy, but I found an unexpected refuge. Just above the first mass of leaves a large bough had torn away from the trunk and had left a great gash in the side of the tree. In an effort to patch itself up the tree had grown numerous thin branches which hid the gash from the ground. I parted them and slipped inside, letting them close over me as I faced outwards. I could see very little despite my vantage point and I was convinced that no one could see me. I heard my pursuer smashing his way through the undergrowth, swearing at the frequent tears and scratches which he was enduring. I looked down, but could see no signs of my footprints on the grass of the glade. I just hoped that he wouldn't climb the tree to see if he could get some sort of view of where I had gone. In that, at least, I was disappointed. He arrived snorting and panting. He looked round at the trees and then became utterly still, listening for any sounds of my progress. He chose my tree to climb to see if the view would be helpful. I shrank back into the recess which held me. I saw his hand on the branch just below my feet when he stopped. There was the sound of the undergrowth being parted and three or four pigeons took off with violent claps of their wings from the branches of a tree which was out of sight. At once he slithered down the trunk and set off towards the noise. From the sound of it a deer was making its way through the wood, but this townie would apparently be unable to distinguish the noise from mine.

As is the nature of woods, it is quite easy to get lost in them. I crouched in the cleft and listened to his progress. He was circling round at some distance from the glade. I heard a mixture of his body crashing through the undergrowth, his stertorous breathing and the frequent swear words when he was caught by some particularly vicious branch. The noises became more distant. I sat down in the cleft and examined my legs. There were one or two congealed drops of blood but almost nothing in the way of serious scratches. My shorts had suffered and there were rips in two places. My T-shirt was filthy, had one hedge tear but was otherwise intact. I felt a slightly painful place on my thumb and found that there was a -roken off thorn embedded in it. I sucked it until the skin was soft and then squeezed it and applied my teeth in order to drag it out. A needle would do the job in seconds, so I gave up.

I listened carefully and could hear nothing. I had a rough idea where the house was, but leading off the glade was a path which avoided the worst excesses of the hawthorn bushes and the brambles. I followed it in what I thought was an approximation of the location of the house and eventually came to the end of the trees. I looked out from behind a bush and was concerned to see a couple of hundred metres away Steven and one of the spare men with a dog tugging at its leash. They had some cloth with them and it was clear to me that they were following a trail. It took several seconds for me to realise that it was my trail into the wood. As they passed out of sight following the eager dog, I dodged towards the house, circled the mews and entered by the door to the back stairs. I sprinted up them and found my room. I found a needle in my bag and extracted the thorn. The next obvious thing to do was to have a shower, change and present myself downstairs and see what the reaction was.

I walked out of the big front doors, turned to the right and found the others looking decidedly scruffy and flustered. Emily was staring at me as if she'd seen a ghost. She narrowed her eyes and asked me where the hell I'd been. I replied that I'd been for a little run and that I thought I ought to look more appropriate for the company. Emily's T-shirt was ripped and filthy, she had grass stains on the seat of her shorts and her hair was a mess. By this time several of the others were crowding round. A spare man told me that Steven and Darren had gone in search of me. I laughed. I had achieved my end which was to outrun my pursuer and then leave him guessing. After Charles and George I didn't want to be caught. Lisa looked as if she had 'suffered' at the hands of her pursuer. Her blouse was ripped and the catch at the waist of her shorts was twisted. She had numerous grass stains on her clothes and skin and looked like a classic case for forensic examination. Only she wouldn't be laying any charges. Charles took out his mobile phone and called Steven. 'She's here,' he told him, 'and looking fresh and lovely.' I felt smug to the point of priggish. What's more I seemed to have been the only woman not caught. The redhead and the blonde were obviously unhappy with my evasion of their fate. The redhead had been wearing a designer T-shirt and shorts, but I doubted if even the most thorough washing and repair work would return them to a wearable condition. The blonde had apparently lost one trainer and had a nasty bruise on her thigh, together with a tear in her T-shirt which just about rendered it superfluous. I sat on a canvas chair and watched the others. Most of the men looked as if they had been over-exerting themselves and I attracted a number of not very friendly glances. I suppose that people can forgive anything but the use of intelligence to obtain success. As I was considering the truth of this, Steven, Darren and the dog arrived, rather out of breath and sweating profusely. They ran up to me, the dog barking loudly. It was the same question, which got the same answer. The reply was not at all what I expected. Steven was overcome by rage, 'You cheated,' he shouted at me. 'You spoiled the game!' He drew a breath. 'You should be punished.' I saw that I was surrounded by those who had stuck to the literal instructions Steven had issued. 'You said nothing about not outwitting my pursuer.' I told him. 'It's not my fault if he is too thick to understand countryside sounds.' This drove Steven to even greater fury.

Steven looked at the assembled group. 'You did your best. She was sly and crafty. What shall we do with her?' There was a cry of 'Punish her.' Suddenly I realised that I was in a precarious position. He turned to me. 'You have a choice, accept your punishment, or pack your bags and never return.' There was considerable approval of this ultimatum. Forty per cent of me wanted to avoid punishment, sixty per cent wanted to see Charles, George and Emily again. I asked what the punishment would be. His reply was terse and to the point. 'Stripped naked and whipped.' I felt a sudden weight in my throat and a buzz between my thighs. I knelt before him, 'Please don't hurt me too much,' I implored. I saw his lip curl, and a bulge appear in his shorts. As I knelt hands seized me and the buttons on my dress were undone. The blonde stood in front of me and reached round me and unhooked my bra. Darren pulled down my thong. My sandals were dragged off my feet and suddenly I was standing in the midst of a hostile group trying with no success to cover my nakedness. I began to protest, but Steven was walking away with an order to 'bring her.' However much I felt in the right the strength of ten or eleven people was more than I could resist. I was propelled towards the side of the lawn. In a moment my ankles were tied to two of the stone edging of the grass and I wobbled with my feet half a metre apart. I looked up and saw hanging from a branch another two ropes that corresponded to those which held my ankles. My wrists were securely fastened to these and I stood for all of them to examine in detail. Steven reserved to himself the right to whip me. Darren produced a plaited whip about a metre long. Steven shook it up and down and it turned out to be far more supple than I had thought. He walked round me flicking the whip so that the keep made my skin tingle. I was not used to pain, especially pain inflicted deliberately, and I gasped as the stings increased in speed and number. The sun was beating down on my face and the front of my body. The group was milling about so that they could take up vantage points to see what Steven was going to do with me. I was all too well aware that I had no protection from any of them and that they could see every crevice and curve of my body, and at least I loved that part. I found out exactly what getting a buzz out of something really implied. I looked down to see the curves of my breasts and the gleaming gold tips of my nipples standing out on them. I was glad that I was so well endowed without being as voluptuous as the redhead. I was delighted that my waist was so small and the slight swell of my belly was contained in the white bone of my hips. For the briefest of moments I looked towards the sun and then all I could see was a purple image of the girl in my dream who was not me then, but now was. I saw the sun reflected on the gold ornaments between her thighs which I had copied and I realised that all the onlookers could see my ritual decorations. I felt that I could swing my body and twist in my bonds so that I would be able to dissipate any pain quite easily. Steven was behind me and to my left. Suddenly I felt the violent sting of the whip across my shoulders. I cried out as the whip burnt its track across my skin and I shook to ease the unexpectedly enduring pain. I sank my head down and saw my breasts jiggling against each other. As I glanced up I saw the evident appreciation and lust on the faces of the men, including Charles, and even on more than one of the women.

The second strike caught me at waist level and I felt the tip of the whip encircle me and catch the side of my belly. For a moment I gasped, trying to fill my lungs with air so that I could relieve my pain with a howl. I couldn't believe how painful the stripe was. Eventually I tensed all the muscles in my body and putting my head back I howled in pain and protest. I felt sure that Steven liked me and that he would not prolong the punishment or hurt me much more than he had already done. I waited for the third strike, my chest heaving with great intakes of air. I clenched my buttocks, reckoning that this was where he would next aim. I was not wrong. The whip seemed to have swung in an arc and the flexible leather curved upwards from my thighs and caught me on the abundant under edge of my tightened buttocks. I heard the breath whistle out of my mouth and involuntarily I bucked my hips, thrusting my pelvis forward and presenting the spectators with a fine view of the cleft between my thighs. I could almost see the glittering gold reflected in their eyes. This time my howl was more nearly a groan.

The next slash seemed to come from my other side. I had not expected Steven to be ambidextrous, nor had I suspected that he would carefully lay on another set of weals to cross over the first. The leather crossed my shoulders from right to left, though I could not work out why the tip was the first point of contact followed by the flexible tail of the whip and then part of the thickly braided handle. I screamed and tears began to form in my eyes, making my vision blur. I swung in my bonds, but although it seemed to please the audience it did little to relieve the instant agony. The sun was hot on my body and sweat had begun to trickle over my skin.

The repeat of the strike to my waist was about as much as I could bear and I wept and cried out. I thought that my pitiful situation might draw some sympathy from the group or Steven, but none was forthcoming. He swept the whip across my buttocks, the report of its impact was like a pistol shot. I could not believe that he was punishing me so viciously. I feared for the next slash, I feared for my erstwhile unmarked skin, I feared that I would be unable to take much more pain and felt a pressure in my throat which made me shiver and gasp and stare into the sky with my head back between my arms. It took me a while to realise that this pose thrust forward my breasts and my cunt. I closed my eyes and tried to picture myself as they could see me. It seemed to me that this was their high spot of the weekend, and what would follow it?

I began to recover from this sixth strike and brought my head up to the vertical, holding it between my pinioned arms. Steven had come to stand in front of me and he was obviously about to free me from my fetters. Only, instead he drew off to my right and I saw his arm and hand with the whip in it swing towards me as if in slow motion. Some ridiculous hope in my mind led me to believe that this was a slowly moving swing and that the effect would be little more than a sting. I was quite misled by my own futile wishes and before I managed to prepare myself the whip cracked across my belly. I would have doubled up with the pain but my imprisoned limbs prevented more than a small movement. I could not cope with the fire generated by the biting leather. I felt myself go limp and I knew that I was about to give myself up to the terror of the whip. I hung, knees slightly bent, awaiting the next devastating cut from the whip. I watched as Steven moved further round from me so that he was standing at almost ninety degrees from my right side. Perhaps he was giving the spectators a better line of sight. I saw his arm and the whip ascend above shoulder height and then sweep down. If it followed its trajectory it would strike the ground, but Steven was cleverer than that and he turned the whip into a flail that dragged up my thighs, caught the bottom of my prominent rib cage and then buried itself in the underside curve of my breasts, thrusting them up my chest and causing them to compress and bounce

I expected this pain to be beyond bearing, but some hidden hormone coursed through my body, making me feel as if I was on some sort of high and dissipating the hideous pain that I knew he was inflicting on me. I knew that I had cried out, but I was beyond hearing myself. I could see that the group was clapping in unison and shouting. With an effort I made out that they were goading Steven on with cries of 'more' and suddenly, as the whip struck me again, just under my breasts, I felt a tightening between my thighs, the beginnings of a weight dragging in my vagina, a fluttering in my belly and I began to hope that he would strike me until I got the release that all these signs portended. I looked Steven in the eye, but all I could see was the hard face of a sadistic workman going about his task with no interest in the body he was excoriating. He seemed to be thinking that I was the least important creature present and that I should serve only as a target for his elegant strikes, designed to inflict the maximum pain and display his muscular physique. I was appalled at his indifference. I was frightened of the bitter smile and concentrated stare as he moved his position and standing in front of me whistled the whip between my thighs and buried it in my cunt. For a moment the world became dark and utterly silent. I must have been shaking because I could hear the tiny sound made as my golden inserts struck one another. There was no other sound, except in the distance a train whistle filling the darkness with its reverberations. Then I realised that the sound was made by me and that I was trying to tramp my feet to reduce the cutting agony if the whip. All at once I became quite light-headed and the pain between my legs was replaced by a great turmoil which began to mount from my belly towards my chest. In the midst of this he struck me again in the same place and then across my breasts. I knew that these blows had left agonising paths, but all my attention was drawn to the passion in my belly and the mounting pressure in my head. As he struck me once more I tilted my cunt towards him, shook my decorated breasts, drew in breath and expanded my ribs until they showed white below the skin, and then I felt the ignition of the climax within me and the sudden gushing of juices from my cunt which wetted my thighs and poured onto the ground in front of me. In reality this was a relief in some seconds, but so great was the deliverance from the mundane world of being thrashed and watched that I felt that I poured out lubricating liquid for some great length of time. I no longer cared what anyone thought of me, I had exceeded even the experience I had enjoyed with George. What I needed was to hang quietly for a while and then to be taken down and feel a strong body holding me in its arms, caressing me and penetrating my bruised vulva.

I hung in the hot sun and slowly returned to some sort of ordinary consciousness. I heard Steven, as if far off, asking if anyone had any use for me, but it seemed that the people were drifting away. Steven instructed Lisa to releases my ankles and then my wrists. I was aware that he was pulling the branch down so that she could reach my hands. She undid my left wrist and I endured the new pain of hanging by one wrist, until she released this one and I fell to the ground, smeared by the churned up mud which I had generated. Steven gave me a parting flick with his whip which stung my breast, but I was too close to unconsciousness even to murmur a complaint, let alone move to protect myself.

I lay naked and grubby in the sun without moving. I could not bring myself to try to stand up. I was lying on my left side with my left arm trapped underneath me and my right forearm resting on my hip. My legs were slightly drawn up with my right knee slightly below the left one. I could hear nothing but the small sound of a bird singing on a branch. I did hear the flutter of its wings as it flew off, and very quickly found what it was that had disturbed it as George's face came into my view. He leaned down towards me and I heard him calling me his poor dear, his poor little thing. He covered me with my dress which he picked up from the ground. I realised that I must be a complete mess. I was dirty, soiled and striped. None of this seemed to concern George who went down on one knee beside me and very gently pushed his hands and forearms under my arms and knees. He started to lift me and I managed to raise an arm and put it round his neck and across his shoulder. I felt very odd. Not so much unwell as not myself.

George told me that I was trembling and held me close, murmuring endearments as he strode away from the punishment zone and round the building towards the mews. The gentle rocking rhythm of his steps lulled me from terror to drifting consciousness. He took me up the stairs to his flat with apparently no effort at all. He opened the door with the hand that was under my knee and kicked it shut behind him. For the first time he lowered my feet to the ground and half dragged, half carried me beyond his bedroom to the bath room. He leaned me against the wall, but my legs would not hold me and I slowly crumpled to the floor. I found myself with my legs folded up under me, resting on my right buttock and with my head pressed against the wall by his shower unit. I was not aware that George had stripped off his clothes and had thrown them in a corner of the bathroom until I again felt the powerful clasp of his muscular arms. He pulled me up to a standing position with a forearm under each of my armpits and lifted me off the ground and propelled me backwards. I could feel the heavy muscles of his chest and belly against my skin and the prod of his engorged cock.

Without being prepared for it I suddenly found myself inundated by a powerful jet of warm water from the shower head. It streamed over my head and face and poured down my chest and over my breasts towards my belly and thighs. It washed over my bruised back and sluiced across and between my buttocks. I could feel every weal that scored my skin, but I was content that George was holding me up and now that he was pouring liquid scented soap over me. I closed my eyes and my mouth and concentrated on the gentle massage of his soapy hands and the rinsing water. I was regaining my strength and lifted my arms to his neck and held myself against him. I felt his mouth on mine and I began trembling again. This was not from pain of fear, but from a desire to hold on to that beautiful, caring man.

He turned off the shower and backed out of the cubicle.

He sat me on a cork-topped chair and reached for a soft white towel. Slowly and gently he dried my hair, my face, my neck, my back and sides, my arms and then my chest and my breasts, working down my belly towards my bruised cunt. He dried my thighs as far as he could and worked on my calves and feet giving my toes a massage all of their own. He carefully lifted me and wrapped me in a vast white bath sheet which covered me from my neck to my ankles. He picked me up again and took me into the bedroom where he softly laid me on the bed, still wholly covered in the white terry-towelling. He covered my feet and ankles with a blanket and kissed me very gently. As he turned away I saw his cock throbbing with its head reared up by his belly. I wanted him, but most of all I wanted him to be close to me and to hold me in his arms.

George returned to the bathroom, but very shortly returned smelling of an expensive deodorant. I murmured that I preferred his own perfume, but the words were stopped by his lips on mine. I caught his arm and pulled him towards me. He lay facing me on the bed and I began to pull the towel away from my now dry skin. What he saw drew a look of consternation from him. I wanted him to hold me, but instead he was fumbling in the bedside cabinet drawer. He squeezed something into his palm and rubbed his hands together. He dripped something onto my skin and then began the sweetest and tenderest massage it was possible to imagine. I drifted in my mind until I saw myself strung up and being beaten. He smoothed the skin of my breasts and I felt again the agonising pain of the whip on my breasts, except that this time it was tempered by the touch of care and perhaps even affection. He turned me over and worked on my back. I was filled with a sensation of floating on some soft cushion wafted along by the gentlest of breezes. He turned me on to my back and began to drizzle the faintly scented oil over my belly. I was beginning to feel the delight of the massage and just a tiny stirring within me. He ran his strong hands across the tops of my thighs and almost imperceptibly opened the lips of my cunt, as he did so pouring a dribble of the slightly warming oil into the folds and crevices and following it with the lightest touch of his fingers. All the time he was telling me how beautiful I was and how they had no right to treat me as they had. I tried to whisper that I had enjoyed being displayed and that the whipping had finally brought me to a totally consuming climax. It was as if he could not hear me.

George half knelt with one knee between my thighs as he quietly fingered me between my thighs. Wonder of wonders I could feel the pain departing and I knew that if he did only a little more of this I would begin the steady pathway to another orgasm. I wanted to have the contact of his skin, I wanted him to penetrate me. With my left hand I pulled at his wrist, as a puzzled look came over his face. This departed very quickly as I seized his cock with my right hand. I looked up into his face and said the one cogent word that he seemed to have heard since he rescued me: 'Please.' George needed no encouragement. He put his other knee between my open thighs and sank his hips until his solid cock was nudging at the entry to my cunt. I was about to guide him in with my hand when I realised that he was in exactly the right place, but that he was using his cock to titillate me and a very good job he was making of it. He supported most of his weight on his arms, but his cock was pressed against me by the weight of the lower part of his belly, the muscular power of his buttocks and the strength of his thighs. Very slowly I felt the tip of his cock begin to penetrate my outer lips. I could visualise just what this big hard shaft looked like and it made me begin to shiver. His pressure was gentle, but inexorable. I felt the head slide into me and pass my inner lips. There was a moment of stillness and then the pressure resumed and I could feel the shaft against the clutching walls of my vagina. He was well on his way to filling me with his cock when he started to withdraw. I could again feel the sliding motion against the membranes of my vulva and was tantalised by the outward movement as much as I had been titillated by the inward. His cock, now well lubricated by his contact with the oil and my gathering juices, was completely withdrawn from me. For some reason I began to count to myself, waiting for the return of the beloved implement. As I got to twelve I again felt the pressure at the gates of my sex, but this time it was a little higher and the tip of his cock touched my clitoris. I felt as if an electric shock had passed through me. At first I put this down to the bruising it had received from the whip, but in a moment I realised that he was working his cock up and down on my pleasure nub catching the inserted ring and that I was gasping for breath. I could feel the beginnings of a flutter in my belly and the risk of another orgasm without him in me. I brought my hips up as far I could and the pressure changed to penetration. This time the lubricants were doing their work and I felt an almost endless pressure and progression as he pushed with infinite slowness into my depths. At last I felt the tip of his cock against my womb and uttered a sigh, opening my legs even further and flinging my arms at right angles to my body. I felt him slowly withdraw and then, at once, push deep into me. I reached up and encircled his thick neck pulling his head down to me. I thought he was going to kiss me but he ducked his head and straining every muscle began to suck my nipples, getting his teeth behind the gold cones which held them.

I found this wonderfully exciting and then realised that I could feel the golden ornaments in my cunt lips pressing against the sides of his cock.

I counted his thrusts until I lost reckoning. He was beginning to make powerful thrusts into me and was grunting with the effort. I could hear my own gasps and the air whistling into my lungs. I knew that even though I was doing my best to hold back my climax, I could do little to delay it much longer and as I looked up into his face I felt the sweat running down his brow dripping onto my shoulder, mingling with the oil and sweat which was coating me. I could stand no more and lay spread-eagled on the bed just concentrating all my consciousness on what this wonderful lover was doing to me. This was the signal for the flutter to become the beating of wings and the arousal of all those emotions and physical emanations which come when a woman gives herself completely to her lover.

I heard George give a great roar and somewhere there was an accompanying high pitched howl. This should have been the greatest sensation I had ever enjoyed, but after a moment I realised it was all too much for me and that my systems had shut down despite the spurting of juices and the mounting tide of passion which was taking me over. I must have gone quite limp by being completely taken over, because the next thing I can remember is lying in George's arms with the blanket covering us up to our necks. I had been loved out of existence. I had enjoyed what every woman wants, to be martyred, saved, cured and loved with a passion wholly for myself alone. In realising what had happened great tears formed in my eyes and I sobbed as if my heart would break. George held me close and tried to comfort me. I don't think he understood when I told him I was so lucky and happy.

In the evening after a refreshing sleep in George's arms

I went to my room and dressed in time for dinner. I chose a satin dress with long sleeves and a mid calf hem line. It was cut high at the throat, but draped beautifully over my body. This was an opportunity not to wear underwear so that the gold cones on my nipples protruded into the fabric and the drape of the material showed up every curve of my body. I wanted to keep my skin away from prying eyes in case they were stimulated to renew the attack on me. I was the last one coming down the stairs to the pre-dinner drinks. I had hardly come into sight of the group of people when I heard the sound of clapping and appreciative comments. All very flattering, I thought, if it was intended for me, but I had seen the naked ferocity in their eyes when I had been whipped in the afternoon. They were sadists, which on reflection was perhaps just as well since I must be a masochist.

As I reached the floor I was surrounded by people telling me how beautiful I was and how brave. They attempted to ply me with drinks, but I refused everything except an apple juice. Charles was there looking rather sheepish, as he might well do given that he had made no attempt to save me from the vicious punishment of the afternoon. I came to the conclusion that there was no one there who I had much desire to know. The visit, and particularly the whipping and its aftermath, had changed me. I knew that I was able to withstand terrible pain, that pain inflicted on me when I was displayed, naked, brought me a reward greater than I had expected. I knew, too, that George was the only one there who cared for me at all. I wondered why I had come to this meal when I would have been happier sharing a can of beans with George.

In the midst of these musings accompanied by looking over the rim of my glass at these people who now seemed embarrassed to look me in the eye, Steven raised his hand and his voice:

'I hope that you have all had a pleasing and enjoyable visit.' He looked everywhere except at me. 'It is about time that I introduced you to your host. In case you wondered, I am not the owner of this elegant house or its beautiful grounds. However, I did arrange this weekend with the help and direction of our host. Some of you may have met him before.'

At this point I was aware of everyone turning to the stairs down which I had recently come. The lights had been dimmed and all I was conscious of was a strongly built man with one hand in his tuxedo trouser pocket coming down the stairs. There was renewed applause which I did not join in. He was at once surrounded by all the people present, but I stood with my glass in my hand and my other hand resting on the back of a chair. I thought I had had enough of this place. I wanted to eat, pack and be ready to leave. There was a good deal of laughter and some very odd comments. I looked at the back of the heads of those nearest to me who included Steven and the spare man who I had misled so recently and so long ago. My eyesight became rather fuzzy. I worked out that I had been traumatised and was very hungry. My blood sugar level must have been extremely low. As I held myself up on the chair arm I was vaguely conscious that the outline of the group was changing and that a figure had detached itself from the others and was coming towards me. It seemed to be the man who had come down the stairs, but it was not until he put his arm round me and kissed me that I was aware that this was George. Another funny joke. But I didn't mind. I knew from everything in his touch and my reaction to him that I loved him, despite the curious hoax he was playing on me.

George in a designer tux, no, I didn't think so. I felt I

was slipping away from everyone, mentally and physically, but I did not fall. A strong arm held me and a commanding voice called for assistance. In a moment I was reclining on a sofa and shortly after that the other people went into the dining room. Only George and a servant remained. I was brought a bowl of soup. Automatically I spooned the broth into my mouth. I felt its warmth run down to my stomach. The empty bowl was removed and a plate was given to me which contained thin slices of what looked like grilled chicken, with a few potato wedges and a small portion of salad. I realised I was achingly hungry and forked the food. My heart beat became slower and more regular, I lifted my eyes to look properly at my saviour. It was indeed George. My head swam. I couldn't understand. Everything felt as if it was beyond me. This George asked me how I felt. I looked at him with disbelief. He smiled at me. He told me that he was the very George who had taught me to fish and had rescued me from the lake, and the same George who had carried me to his rooms. I stuttered out an incomprehensible series of questions, but he did no more than smile at me and asked if I had eaten enough. I stood up, very shakily. George picked me up and carried me to the stairs which he mounted effortlessly. The servant preceded us and opened the door of my room. There was a woman in a maid's uniform who was neatly folding my clothes and was putting them in my case.

George asked me if I was ready to go. I asked him about Lisa and Emily and he assured me that they would find their own way home. The four of us descended the stairs and with rapidly increasing strength and bewilderment George led me out of the door. Before us was a beautiful dark green Bentley. He helped me into the back seat and joined me. He pressed a button and an opaque screen separated us from the driver. George issued brief instructions and before I knew it we were underway.

During the journey George explained his preference for a quiet life. He had a little flat in town. He asked if I would like to visit. We arrived at what I vaguely recognised as the Nash terraces overlooking Regent's Park. The car came to a silent halt and the chauffeur was out of his seat and had George's door open and then mine. The three of us entered the darkened building through a garden glimmering with scented blossom. The door opened at the chauffeur's palm print and we went in to find a large reception hall with a lift beside the beautiful staircase. We took the lift and came out at the top floor and the chauffeur tripped the lights as he preceded us. He threw back double doors and George ushered me through into a huge room, bathed in light. For a moment I stood still, taking in my surroundings. It all seemed vaguely familiar with elegant furnishings, an outlook onto the Park, and settees at right angles to the fireplace which contained a huge grate of ceramic coals heated by a gas fire. I looked around. There was an oak table and twelve oak chairs which would have dwarfed the average room. To one side there was an Emperor size divan covered by a Chief Joseph rug of intricate and wonderful pattern. In one corner there was a desk with a computer and a flat screen monitor on a desk with a cabinet beside it, illuminated by a standard lamp. I looked up. There were two lighting gantries which extended across the ceiling. Only one was lit, with lights pointing in all directions and suffusing the room with a golden glow.

George conducted me to a bedroom with an en suite bathroom. He told me that if I would like to stay this would be my room. My case was on a low bench and in the two minutes of our stay in the sitting room had been unpacked. Even if George hadn't pressed me to stay, someone had made it difficult to refuse, as if I wanted to.

By the time I had returned to the big room the chauffeur had departed and George had settled himself with a magazine by the fire. He stood up as I came in and invited me to sit opposite him. I lay back in the soft cushions and looked up at the ceiling where the lights largely obscured the gantry on which they were mounted. He told me that all sorts of tricks could be performed at the press of a button. I was sure that they could, but tomorrow would be a better day.

Dear John,

I promised that I would write to you when we parted. Fortunately, I have my laptop with me and so I will e-mail this so that you get it as soon as I have finished it. I must say that the travelling has been pure pleasure. Dr Nicholas has had the yacht fitted out to the highest possible standard with every hi-tech device you can think of and the furnishings and appointments are of wonderful quality with mahogany and polished brass everywhere. Although it is called a yacht it has a very powerful engine and cuts relentlessly through the water at great speed. It does have sails and masts, but the latter are used for the entertainment of the passengers, not, as you might have expected, so that they can climb to the top and look out over the sea, though that opportunity is there, but so that any defaulting member of the crew can be tied to the polished wood and punished for whatever misdemeanour it is that has been committed. The crew is half men and half women, just like the passengers. The women passengers and crew members seem to be much more attractive than the men, though the crew can boast some fine physical specimens. The male passengers seem mostly to be elderly men associated with trophy wives or mistresses.

During the afternoon of each day the yacht stops and they lower thick nets over the side so that we can swim in the sea for an hour or so. I have made very good use of the bikini which you gave me, though I must say that it is just a bit small for me. That's all right for the bottom half because I have been totally waxed and the cord between my buttocks disappears almost completely. The bra has led me to be quite careful when I move about as it only just covers my nipples and any abrupt movement leads to a good deal of fall out. Swimming is OK, but climbing the boarding net gives the onlookers a very good view of the whole of my breasts. Still, the men seem to appreciate it, and I have already received one or two offers relating to what they seem to think is my need for protection.

In the evening the yacht slows and we have a dance. Dr Nicholas seems to have a vast collection of dressing up clothes, so we are able to have a fancy dress dance whenever we feel like it. Last night I went as a Latin American dancer. You can guess that my costume was almost as revealing as your bikini. Not only was the skirt so short that its hem hardly covered the sparkling thong I wore underneath it, but the top was of some clinging material which was virtually transparent as well as being very abbreviated. Like the skirt it had glittering beads on streamers attached to it, so that when I spun round they flew up to the horizontal, which got me some approving comments. I wore those gold strappy sandals with the ten centimetre heels, which showed off my leg muscles and forced me to tilt my pelvis in a most inviting way. You'll be pleased to know that I refused three invitations to visit staterooms.

Dr Nicholas seems preoccupied with the management of the ship, or some business deal, but we're told he will put in appearance tomorrow.

I do hope that you are managing without me, I miss you very much.

Love and Kisses,

Laura.

Dear John,

Of course I'm not deliberately showing off my body to be ogled at. Remember this was your choice of a trip for me. The dress rules here seem to be that as little as possible is the order of the day. You can be quite comforted by knowing that at last night's dance some of the passengers decided to provide a little cabaret. One gorgeous coffee-coloured lady demonstrated the art of belly dancing. She was utterly magnificent. Her face looks like a Benin bronze with wonderfully chiselled features. Her hair was oiled and drawn back from her face and had ropes of jewels twisted into it. The tiny scrap of veil she was wearing caught into her hair just above her ears did nothing to conceal her face, but threw her eyes into great prominence. She had the most beautiful dark brown, almost liquid looking eyes, topped by slender arched eyebrows and a nose which seemed to belong to the most exquisite Greek statue. High cheekbones were echoed by a mouth of perfect fullness and symmetry, which hid teeth of dazzling whiteness and a curling tongue that occasionally protruded deliciously between them. She hadn't bothered with a bra and showed off her wonderful conical breasts with large dark areolas and long nipples to which she had clipped strands of jewels that shone with a scintillating fire. Her waist was unbelievably tiny, I am sure you could have encompassed it with your hands, and knowing you, you'd certainly have wanted to try!

Her hips flared out from her waist and slung across them was a skirt made up of separate strands of gold thread, each one carrying brilliant beads. The waist band of the skirt was caught up on one hip, but came well down towards her thigh on the other side. She was barefoot and moved with a wonderful grace into the middle of the little dance floor. There was a small group of musicians who seemed to be well prepared for the show and played some exotic music to suit the girl's actions. She started off by walking slowly round the tables by the dance floor, shaking her breasts and making the muscles in her belly go into a series of contractions which opened and closed her decorated navel and made me think that she would lose the skirt at any moment. At the end of the circuit she moved to the centre of the dance floor and raised her hands above her head, interlacing her fingers with the backs of her hands together. She then began the belly dance with considerable passion. She had the most remarkable control over the muscles of her belly, seemingly being able to move them both laterally and vertically. As she performed she began to turn, slowly at first, with the strands of the skirt parting over her thighs and then jerking her breasts by drawing in the muscles just alongside her arm pits. The turning became faster and her skirt began to fly up as she moved. I thought it was my imagination until I realised that her skirt was all that she wore below her waist and that she was displaying her naked cunt, which like mine had been waxed, so that her furled lips gleamed in the reflected beam of the spotlight, enhanced by her beaded skirt. There were only momentary glimpses as she turned and shook, but after a few moments in which she gathered appreciative applause from all those present, she reached down to her waist band and detached the fastening in a single pull, holding the skirt before her as a kind of stage prop and then swinging it round in a great arc, showing us all her perfect body. She bent forward with her legs slightly apart and the skirt draped over her shoulders, until her head nearly touched the floor, then she slowly drew herself up with her feet now further apart, and began to lean back until in a display of wonderful muscular control, her hands hovered above the floor and then touched it, still holding the waist band of the skirt, which was spread out behind her head. The tautness of her now naked body threw every muscle into relief, and I was sure that the men were only just about controlling their desire to rush on to the floor, seize her by the hips and plunge themselves into her. The applause was even louder than before, but she was not finished. She edged her legs back towards her hands so that she was narrowing still further the angle of her body. Her mouth opened and she began to breathe through it with her tongue protruding. As she slowly drew herself into the narrowest of angles her legs seemed to open further and I could see that the place between her thighs was glistening. Suddenly she began to contract the muscles of her belly, shake her breasts and utter a series of rasping gasps. I am sure that some of the audience thought that she had done too much and had hurt herself, but I recognised the grunts and the open knees as evidence of her approach to an orgasm. The contraction of her bottom pressed her cunt upwards and I longed to put my head between her thighs and suck her into the orgasm that was now inescapable. Instead I watched with fascination as she cried out and juices spurted from her open cunt, running down her thighs and the crease of her buttocks. She let out a howl and slowly subsided into a heap, drawing the skirt over her, but singularly failing to cover herself at all effectually.

A uniformed member of the crew stepped forward and looked down at her. He announced that she had overstepped the mark and that tomorrow she would be punished.

The rest of the cabaret was amusing, but had nothing like the impact of the belly dancer. I had seen her before, dressed in a demure uniform, doing some semi-domestic chore on the cabin deck, but whoever could have guessed that such a quiet girl would turn into this ravishing passionate woman?

I hope you have enjoyed my account of the evening's entertainment. I will let you know what happens tomorrow.

As ever, all my love

Laura

Dear John,

I am sorry that you have been so busy at work. You City types certainly earn your six figure bonuses. I am glad you liked the story of the belly dancer. I shall ask her for some lessons in a few days, though I don't think I could do anything like the finale, apart that is from coming, and only if you were there to help me.

Today Dr Nicholas put in an appearance at breakfast. I don't know what I had expected, but I was surprised. Physically he's of medium height, but strongly built. He has what I can only imagine is prematurely grey hair which is neatly combed, and a goatee beard and moustache hides the lower part of his face. I really can't work out how old he is, but he radiates confidence and power. I don't need to tell you what great aphrodisiacs these two are, even in an otherwise unattractive man, and Dr Nicholas is definitely not unattractive. We were all enjoying a fine breakfast when he stood up and introduced himself. He apologised for not being with us up to the present, hoped that we had been enjoying ourselves and promised that things would be even more enjoyable in the future. At this point he broke off as the uniformed officer from the previous night whispered to him. "I understand," he said, "that one of the crew exceeded the requirements of her duty last night." There was some laughter and clapping. "I like to keep a tight ship, and whilst I am only nominally captain I agree with Captain Thorn, that this member of the crew should be punished in the traditional seaman's way. This will be in an hour's time on deck. After the punishment she will be available to any member of the passengers who wishes to continue the punishment in whatever way they seek. Crew members are very well paid on this ship and are hand picked for their skills and accept that they may be subject to punishment. All available crew will be mustered for the formal punishment." I had no idea what to expect, but I changed into a georgette top and that pair of shorts which are cut up the sides almost to the waist band. With everyone else I wandered onto the deck and followed the group towards the main mast.

There was an officer, a crew member I recalled seeing in the engine room on my tour of the ship, and dressed in what seemed to be a shapeless tube of white cloth, fastened at the shoulders, stood the belly dancer of the previous night with her eyes cast down. The officer told us that it was the tradition to punish all miscreants in the same way, regardless of rank, age or sex. The Captain had decreed that this punishment should be moderate and that it should be delivered by the Master at Arms so that she should remember that her display was for the pleasure of the audience and not her own. Of course, should we have wished her to exhibit her pleasure, that would have been quite a different thing. So, the nakedness, the wonderful eroticism and her display of herself in the amazing pose were all acceptable, but her orgasm wasn't. Unless we asked for it. But how did we ask for her to display herself in the first place? I'd no idea, but I thought I'd better get to know the organising committee.

There was a roll of drums and the officer shouted, "Strip her!" The Master at Arms loomed over the girl and reached for the fastenings at her shoulders. Her face was downcast and remained so as the tube of cloth fell down her body revealing her to be naked underneath it. The officer said "Lower," and from a horizontal bar there descended a heavy beam of wood to which was attached a coarse net supported by another beam hanging from the end of several ropes. The vertical distance between the two beams was about three metres and the net was just about square. The Master at Arms said something to the girl and she stepped up on to the lower beam. He said something else and she moved her legs apart and paralleled this with her arms. Someone from the other side of the net appeared to have clipped her wrists and ankles to the ropes of the net. My eyes were fixed on her beautiful back, her narrow waist and her wonderfully curvaceous arse. This was already a wonderful display, but more was to come.

She was left there for several minutes whilst she was asked if she was prepared to take the punishment decreed for her. I heard her almost whispered "Yes," and saw her waist narrow further and her ribs show beneath her skin as she took a deep breath, which I suspected was intended to ward off the tears which her present position seemed to justify, particularly as the front of her body was pressed hard against the rough rope of the net.

I had never seen anyone exhibited like this before. I had most certainly never seen anyone whipped. When I realised what was to happen to her I felt a great lump in my throat and a strange and unexpected feeling between my thighs. I had no idea whether to feel upset and sympathetic for her, or to think that she must have deserved it, or, quite out of character, to look on and enjoy her punishment. The Master at Arms drew a cat o'nine tails from his belt and ran his fingers through the thongs. He drew back his arm and the thongs of the whip trailed out as he struck home towards her back. I saw the thongs spread out over her skin and then fall away. She let out a scream of pain and thrust her body against the net. I moved a little to my right so that I could see her face as well as the strikes to her body. I was in time to see the second blow as it swept up to slash against her buttocks. She howled again and I saw her slam her body against the rough net, her beautiful breasts pushing between two of the rope squares. I saw her mouth open and her eyes close as she howled again. The third strike was to the area just below her armpits and I saw that the Master at Arms had lengthened his strike so that the ends of the thongs curved round her body and the tips struck home at her ribs and her right breast. If her earlier cries had been penetrating, this one was almost deafening. The scream mounted to a sharp crescendo and then continued longer than I'd have thought possible on one lungful of breath.

I had no idea how many of these strikes she had to endure, but I saw the weals begin to develop on her café-au-lait skin as evidence that the Master at Arms was sparing no effort to inflict the maximum pain.

He slashed again at her gorgeous bottom, and once again she thrust herself against the ropes of the net and cried out in pain and despair. She tipped her head back and opened her mouth and I watched her shake and cry out. During the pause between the strikes I wondered what it would be like to be stripped naked and displayed before everyone on the ship and then thrashed. I ought to have been appalled at the thought, but I suddenly realised that I would not wholly mind changing places with the girl, since she was attracting a great deal of appreciative attention and comment. I suppose there is something of the exhibitionist in me which has hitherto lain dormant. As the Master at Arms continued his work I became conscious that I was becoming distinctly sticky around the top of my thighs and that my shorts were inadequately hiding a developing dampness.

After ten strikes to her back, buttocks and thighs the Master at Arms stood back and the sailor who had clipped her wrists and ankles to the ropes of the net, unclipped them and turned her round to face us before securing her again with her back to the net. I thought she was beautiful last night, but in the hot sunlight she seemed to be in the natural state for a girl with such a wonderful figure. It was sheer waste to cover up such a stunning body, and hanging from her wrists on the crude net she looked utterly irresistible. I realised that so far I had felt no sympathy at all for her. In fact I was slightly jealous of her opportunity to be displayed and whipped. She had no chance to do anything but reveal every curve and hidden place of her naked body and to realise that every eye was upon her, nearly all with pleasure and delight, some with envy and many with lust and desire. It was exactly what a beautiful woman wants, but feels that she should never offer. Since she was being punished she had the excuse of being forced into revealing herself, which otherwise might have been pure wantonness. Her performance of the night before was a thing of great beauty, but her own excitement at the display of her body was the reason for this punishment. I wished that I might have done both, but as a passenger travelling alone, I realised that this was quite impossible.

The Master at Arms gave the girl two more strikes, one across the belly and the second upwards between her open legs, scraping the thongs against her thighs and burying them in her cunt. There was a pause before she was able to gather her breath. She opened her mouth and gulped in a great draught of air. I watched as her belly swelled slightly and then her waist narrowed and her chest expanded and her head began to fall back against the ropes of the net with her mouth open and a howl of agony and fear drowning out every other sound on the ship. She bowed her body so that her hips pushed forward and I noticed that her very slightly opened cunt was gleaming with the polish of her own juices. She repeated the cry again and again in decreasing volume as she thrust her hips towards us and shook her breasts together. I realised that it was a cry of pain and of frustration and that she was doing her very best to make herself come.

The officer declared the formal part of the punishment was over, and told us that she must stay just as she was for an hour and then any passenger who thought that the punishment should be continued could do so in the next four hours. The sun beat down on her as the passengers and crew drifted away. I stayed and watched her. I glanced at my watch. It was ten forty. I sat on a neat coil of rope and staked my claim to be the first to continue with her. I expected the men on board to be queuing to abuse her body, but I had not counted on the loyalty of the crew members to one another, nor the powerful influence of the women passengers on their male companions. Sufficient to say that I was on my own at eleven thirty five and thought that I might start operations.

She had watched me, as I had watched her, during the hour after the whipping had ceased. I had sat on the rope coil in the shade but she had been completely exposed to the burning sun. I got up and walked towards her. She gave me a tremulous smile. I told her that I thought she was beautiful and ran a finger down the side of her face and whispered it across her lips. She shook and her breasts jiggled most invitingly. I asked her if she was afraid of me and she said that I had the right to do anything I wanted to her. It didn't answer my question, but it gave me an excuse, not that I felt I needed one. I have never touched a member of my own sex lasciviously, but I thought that I knew just what it was she needed, and I was all too pleased to give it to her. I kissed her unresisting lips and stroked her breast, made slick by the sweat that the sun made trickle down her body. I gently teased her nipple. I could feel the weight of her breast increase and the nipple grow longer and firmer in my fingers. I stood in front of her and continued to work on her breast and her mouth whilst I slowly trailed my free hand down her side and then across her belly, pressing my thumb into her navel. She squirmed and shook and I drifted my fingers down her belly and brushed across the top of her thighs, touching her mons en route, which made her gasp. I could not resist holding off for a while, and so I slipped my hand round her buttock and squeezed it, feeling my fingers close to her nether crater. She pushed down on my hand as far as she was able, but I released my grip and put my hand on her hip, stroking the slightly ridged skin where the whip had scored her. I slid my hand over her belly and down her thigh as far as I could reach and as I released her mouth from mine she began to make little noises like a kitten calling for its mother to suckle. I thought it was time to go to work on her and I pressed my fingers upwards, opening her vulva, inserting three fingers in her vagina and using my thumb to search out and then massage her clitoris. I looked into her face and the effect of my hands working on her was electrifying. I bent my head to suck

126

the breast and nipple that I had not attended to so far, and out of the corner of my eye I could see the muscles of her belly rolling and contracting and very shortly the discharge of the first juices which had gathered to lubricate her and then, suddenly, I heard a long drawn out moan and she began to spurt juice in a strong stream.

I decided to punish her by continuing my manipulation even after she had come. I was keen to see how many times I could make her come and what the effect might be. I looked into her face, which seemed to indicate her movement into a trance of satisfied desire but I was not to be put off and continued to use my fingers on both her breasts and to continue with what had pleased her between her legs. She began to gasp, but she made no effort to plead for mercy. I increased the rate of my massaging of her vulva, becoming conscious of her renewed passion and of my own excitement which was causing me to trickle juice down my thighs. She was not the only one who was gasping, but I had no means of doing anything for myself as a couple of spectators had arrived and were watching the tableau in front of them.

I got myself into a position where I could suck her right breast whilst with one hand I tweaked and pulled the nipple of the left one and my other hand was buried deep inside her with my thumb still rubbing against her clitoris. I decided that I would withdraw two fingers from within her and see if I could find the brown bud between her buttocks. I was most fortunate that my well lubricated fingers almost at once found their target and started to penetrate her. Her body at once stiffened as if something very hot had entered her, but I pressed on and felt her sphincter part under the pressure of my fingers and heard her gasping above my shoulder. As far as she could she pressed her hips downward to make it easier for me to penetrate her, and I knew that she was close to another orgasm. Had I been devoted to punishing her I would then have stepped back, leaving her completely frustrated, but as it was I admired her beauty and her fortitude under the whip and her response to me. I continued entering her as far I could and was suddenly aware of a weight on my shoulder. Her head was close to mine and her lips and teeth were nibbling at my skin. There was nothing but affection and the desire to return delight in this gesture, but it added such a charge to my feelings about her that the knot which had formed between my thighs abruptly unravelled. There was an intense pulsing in my belly and as I caught her juices in my palm and heard the beginning of her orgasmic howl, I must have cried out myself and I spurted into my shorts which provided no camouflage and my own juices ran down my thighs and dripped onto the deck.

I was appalled by the reaction of what were now half a dozen onlookers who cheered and clapped at our joint climax. I stepped back from the girl and was immediately clasped by a large man who held me close to him with one big hand on my breast and the other on my belly. He told me he was going to fuck the belly dancer, but that he would much rather come to my cabin and make love to me. I squirmed out of his grip and to the laughter of the members of his group, I ran off to find the companionway to my cabin.

So you can see that I have developed new skills and discovered new desires that I was unaware that I possessed. I can't wait to get back to you so that we might try out one or more of these new delights, perhaps at Charles's country house parties?

All my rather frustrated love,

Laura

Dear John,

You are right, I have no idea how I came to be an envious onlooker at the barbarity that was being inflicted on that beautiful girl, nor do I understand how it is that I was quite so turned on by the whole affair, or managed to inflict my own 'punishment', though I doubt that is what she would have called it. I think I deserve several gold stars for evading the large man and his rampant cock, though I must tell you that I would have given a lot to be penetrated, but only by you.

The cruise has continued much as before, but I have been very careful to wear modest clothing and implicitly deny whatever story the onlookers may have told about me.

Tonight there is a dance, but I might well make an excuse and retire to bed.

As ever, I shall think of you in my arms.

Laura.

Dear John,

At the bar yesterday evening I met a very striking woman, called Venetia, who told me that she was the chair of the passengers' entertainments committee, and as I was a young woman on my own, perhaps I'd like to join, and perhaps I'd like to put forward some ideas of my own, which they might do their best to put into effect. You can well imagine the turmoil within me. I knew just what it was that I wanted, but I didn't think that I had any chance of it being put on, and in any case I was too ashamed to ask. Instead I asked her how they had got the coffee-coloured girl to perform, and had they approved of her nakedness. She told me that many members of the crew had skills quite unconnected with their maritime duties and that she had a list if I would like to see it. I can hardly wait.

I asked her if it would be possible to have lessons in belly dancing and she said that it could easily be arranged. The belly dancer is apparently called Miria and she is only too willing to share her expertise. Within a few minutes it was arranged, so that instead of going to the dance I was to learn an entirely new one from the beautiful Miria.

I was pleased to get away from the group as a whole and in any case I wanted to talk to Miria and ask her about the punishment and what she thought of my part in it.

I had a very light evening meal and presented myself at the work-out room. I had no idea what to wear, so I put on my red crop top and hung that Indian skirt from my hips. A pair of sneakers and a Gossard thong completed my ensemble. As it happened I could have gone in jeans and a T shirt. Miria was already there and was wearing her demure uniform. This was not at all what I was expecting, but we smiled rather shyly at one another and she invited me to sit down. We tacitly agreed to avoid the subject of her punishment and the reason for it, at least for the time being.

She explained that belly dancing required a great deal of muscular development and control and also that it was intended to attract the eye of the viewer, to titillate and finally to satisfy. She asked me if I wished to learn belly dancing as it had originally been practised in the classical period, or whether I would prefer the somewhat more plastic version, complete with coverings that remained in place, which had been designed for the nineteenth and twentieth centuries. I thought for a moment, recalled her wonderful display at the cabaret, and thought of you. I am sure that like everything else in your life, you would prefer the real thing.

She told me that the preparation before the dance was designed to ensure that the dancer was in the mood for the display she was about to give. Laid out over a bench was the outfit which she had worn during her performance and another which I had not seen before and which I couldn't quite fathom. Miria took off her jacket and then her blouse. She said that she would make herself up and then me. I stared at her body and wondered if I could come anywhere near being as beautiful and erotic as she was. I sat next to her and took off my crop top. She told me I had beautiful breasts and looking in the mirror I saw that ours were very similar in size and shape. I told her I was proud mine seemed to be like hers but that I longed to be the same colour as she was. She laughed and told me that she longed to be pink and white.

I watched as she made up her eyes with thick purple eye shadow and black mascara and then carefully outlined her full lips with dark red lipstick. In only two or three minutes the effect was stunning, but she was not finished and she made up her nipples and areolae with a touch of the eye shadow. She turned to me and told me that she would make me up to suit my blonde hair so the eye shadow was mauve blended into the black of the mascara, but she cleverly avoided making me into a panda. The soft touch of the brush around my eyes and the pressure of the lipstick made me feel positively weak at the knees and a little pulse seemed to be working in my belly as she brushed my nipples with the makeup brush. I looked in the mirror and saw that she had emphasised my mouth and my eyes and that I looked almost as languorously erotic as she did. I must say I was surprised, especially when she grasped my right breast which instantly became heavy and erected my nipple even further. She took a clip from the drawer and opened it against the spring and let the teeth grasp my nipple. The slight pain stirred me even further and I looked in the mirror to see the lines of beaded threads adorning the lower part of my breast. She did the same for my other breast and I was very pleased with the effect. She held up the two clips which had adorned her when she performed for us and invited me to attach them. I was not as deft as she was and probably caused her more pain than she inflicted on me, but her sole response was to run her thumb over my nipples which gave me a fiery sensation. She put on the tiny wisp of veil and then fitted mine. I had never worn anything like it before, but I must say the effect was quite remarkable. I could still see my features, but my eyes seemed to have been greatly emphasised. The original intention might have been to disguise the dancer, but the effect for both of us was strangely alluring.

She stood up and kicked off her shoes, pulled at the fastener of her skirt and stood in front of me with just the tiniest of thongs hiding her pussy. I slipped out of my sneakers and undid the Velcro closure of my waist band and stepping out of my skirt I hung it over the back of the chair. My thong was jewelled and Miria said how much she liked it. She removed hers and I saw again the pretty fold of her cunt, bare of any adornment. I took off my thong and watched as she put on her skirt of threads. It hung like an insecure curtain across her hips and belly, only the swell of her buttocks stopped it from slipping down her legs. She pulled it up and showed me the line of wig tape which kept it attached to one hip.

She handed me the costume which she had brought for me, holding it up by its narrow tape which constituted the waist band. It was a shimmering strip of some silky cloth but only about eight centimetres wide. I looked at it with some concern. She told me that it was her display cover and that I should put it on with the dangling strip at the front. I pulled the waistband tight round my waist, but Miria told me that it was intended to be worn as low over the hips as was possible and that it relied on my buttocks to keep it in place. She undid the waist band and lowered it until the upper line was just a centimetre above my mons. I felt very exposed and wondered if I could keep the thing in place.

She held her hands above her head as she had done before. She told me that this elongated her body and displayed it to the audience without endangering the security of the skirt. I stood before the mirror and adopted the same pose. I didn't have the benefit of the sticky tape in my waist band and the stretch pulled in my bottom just sufficiently for the skirt to slip a little down my belly until the waist band settled at a point just below the crease in my labia. I was about to reach down and pull it up but she stopped me, telling me that this was just how it should be. The narrow panel dangled between my calves and I realised that its hem was weighted so that it would fly up if I spun round.

Miria taught me how to shake my breasts, both with my hands above my head and joined in front of me. We then came to the technique of shaking my breasts and my belly. She told me that, ideally, I should be a bit plumper, but when it came to rolling my muscles I was surprised that I could do it quite well and that when I relaxed I could manage to shake my belly, even though I felt a vague uneasiness that I was about to lose my covering. We twisted and turned together, rolled our bellies and shook our breasts. It was great exercise, but I must admit that I wanted an audience whose members would be stimulated by the sight of my almost naked body and who might gain occasional glances between my thighs as my cover drifted in the centrifugal movement when I spun round.

The music was played from a tape and made me work twice as hard. Miria told me how good it was to gain total control of my pelvic floor muscles and that a number of sessions would tone them so that I might fiercely grip anything introduced into my vagina. I liked that idea very much. She asked me if I would like to try doing a crab, which is a rather more gentle version of her finale. I thought that was a fine thing to be able to do, and I raised my arms above my head and began to bend backwards. Miria stood at my side and put her arm under the small of my back so that I could not fall over. I felt the strain on the muscles of my thighs and belly, but I was confident that Miria would save me from falling. I found the touch of her body distinctly stimulating. At last my hands touched the floor behind me and my body was as taut as I thought was possible. I was wrong because, still holding me with her left arm, Miria drummed her fingers on my belly, starting at my navel and moving slowly towards the tape round my hips. This was a very enjoyable sensation, though I wanted her to do more. She told me to walk my heels back towards my hands, and I very slowly moved them so that I became even more narrowly bowed. At the apex of my curve, Miria continued to hold me with her left arm, although my hands and feet were well spread out, but her right hand was stroking my breasts and her thumb and forefinger were pulling at my nipples. I was just beginning to gasp with the effort of the crab, but this attention made me draw in my breath and then give a little cry. Miria bent her head down towards my face and told me that she owed me, and asked if this would be a good time to repay her debt.

Her fingers were touching the cover strip where it hung between my thighs. I found I could not answer her. The blood pounded in my inverted head and I could feel the familiar knot forming in my belly. She flicked the strip away from between my thighs and at once I felt her fingers gently opening my labia and pressing inside me. Her thumb at once found my pleasure bud and she worked on me with wonderful skill. My position was becoming painful and I was gasping. Half of my mind wanted to stop and lie down, but after I caught sight of us both in the mirror all my body wanted her to continue until I fell into oblivion. I was in no doubt about my desire for control of the muscles of my belly. I could feel my pelvic floor muscles contracting and squeezing Miria's fingers. She seemed pleased, but this was nothing to what I felt as she laid her heavy breasts on my belly and increased the speed and pressure of the massage she was giving me between my thighs. I wanted to reach up and fondle her breasts and then put my hand into her as I had done before, but I heard her telling me to take all that she was giving me and enjoy it as much as I could. This amounted to an almost total loss of hearing and sight. All I could do was feel. The wings beat in my belly, the knot again unravelled, but this time it was my turn to spurt in a pulsing stream into her hand. I think I must have cried out, because the next thing I knew was Miria kneeling beside me on the floor, kissing my lips and telling me I was beautiful. In our case honours were about even.

After some minutes of affectionate caresses and kisses we used cold cream to remove our make up and dressed in our usual clothes. We have agreed to meet again tomorrow morning for another lesson.

Life, as you will have noticed, has become much more interesting.

You are certainly in for a good time when I get home.

All my love

Laura

Dear John,

I'm very surprised. I thought you might want to know exactly what I had been doing. I am sure you wouldn't want me to lie or keep secrets. The very fact that I can tell you in great detail surely indicates that I am both honest and faithful to you. Believe me, if I wanted to stray there is every opportunity on this boat. The relationship between Miria and me is purely one of pleasure. I don't suppose that you want me to go without any delight. After all, you told me that when I was away from you last time you used to go to bed and take your beautiful cock in your hand and think of me and very slowly make yourself come. Since Miria and I have no emotional baggage, I can't think that it could be any different. Just think about it, or I will not tell you of my second and third sessions learning belly dancing with Miria.

Love

Laura.

Dear John,

I do understand your feelings. It must be very frustrating for you to know that I am achieving at least a limited amount of satisfaction whilst you are left on your own. Still, as I say, honesty is the best policy and you warned me that I would come back from this voyage a changed woman. I just hope you like the change. I am sure that I have far more to learn, but something new happens every day and I am surprised at my reaction to it. Because you have explained your feelings, and because you have understood mine, and I understand yours, I will continue to tell you what is happening on the yacht and if it involves me. I will tell you now that I miss you dreadfully and that nothing is better than being held close in your arms. However, you will have to take account of the fact that you wanted me to change and perhaps that is happening; or it might just be the strangeness of the yacht and the long periods of idleness and self indulgence.

This morning I met Miria shortly after breakfast. This time we didn't wear the belly dancing costumes, but we stripped to our thongs. Had I known this was what she had in mind I would have worn a rather more concealing scrap of material. It was more a striptease artist's excuse for a cover, something more like a string than a thong. Miria didn't seem to mind, and her own was hardly an effective cover being held in place by the slenderest of elastic threads. She demonstrated the movement from knees to chest. Nearly all of this is sideways, to match the shaking of the breasts which she seemed able to roll against each other, a technique she also promises to teach me. She pointed out that the whole process had to be titillating, but wasn't intended to simulate sex, except that every so often the dancer gives a random thrust of her hips whilst standing with her feet apart, but this is so quick that the members of the audience are convinced that what they see is wishful thinking. She assures me that it turns both men and women on. Rolling the muscles of my belly is extremely hard work, but I am sure that you will appreciate the action when we are together again.

I had a further gruelling session this afternoon and because it is all one to one training I feel I am making very rapid progress. Tomorrow Miria is going to show me how to manipulate my skirt and also how to manage my finale. If this goes on I shall have an entirely new career opening up before me!

I had lunch with Venetia who told me that the entertainments committee would meet at 2 p.m. which would give me an hour and a half before I was due to see Miria. Venetia asked me if I was enjoying the lessons and I told her that they were doing me the world of good. She asked what we wore and I told her that it was very little. She seemed increasingly interested, but it was close to the time for the meeting. I was introduced to the others who included the officer who had superintended Miria's punishment, a very distinguished looking elderly gentleman who greeted me very warmly and who I, rather embarrassed, later recalled was one of the onlookers at my 'punishment' of Miria. There was another woman, perhaps five or six years older than me, with a low cut top and some devastating cleavage to go with her auburn hair and well-tanned skin. This was Caroline. The older man was George, the officer addressed him as Sir George, but he told him that just his first name would be better. I didn't catch the officer's name, and didn't like to ask again. I can find out from Venetia. There were numerous suggestions for evening activities, and I was quite surprised at some of them. I thought that a game of cards would be a fairly innocuous way of passing an hour or so, but I then picked up that it wasn't Whist or Bridge that they had in mind, but Poker, and strip Poker at that. I was about to raise an objection when I thought that after all, it might not be a bad idea. A good way to see more of my fellow passengers! Another fancy dress dance was proposed, but this time the costumes were to be from the red wardrobe, no doubt to make a change from the last time.

Caroline suggested a fashion show with various classes including smartest, most suitable for the Mediterranean, swimming costumes and then, most daring. I reckoned Miria's display kit would be hard to beat. Another cabaret night was proposed and Venetia was particularly asked to invite Miria to participate. She smiled at me and told the others that there might be a new dancer for their enjoyment. They all seemed pleased and I felt a blush ascend from my neck. Not like me to blush, but if both of us were to perform...well, the sky would be the limit. "I'd like to see some striptease," said George, "and so would I," Caroline agreed. We thought that all we had to do now would be to arrange which night was for which entertainment and then publicise the events and where necessary, ask for performers in events which didn't involve everyone's active participation. However, the officer raised some questions. The first was whether crew members could be in the audience or participate. That was easily dealt with and the unanimous vote was for both. He then raised the matter of the treatment of participants in competitive events. He reminded us all of the punishment of a woman crew member and the reasons for it. There was no problem with the crew, he pointed out, but what sanctions might we wish to impose on a passenger, who, for instance, cheated at cards. The end of this discussion was that we were all on the ship together and if found to have committed a misdemeanour, should be treated alike. I quivered at the thought and hoped that I could think of some offence that I could commit.

As I said, the session with Miria was very strenuous and my thighs and belly ached afterwards. At the end of it we sat on the sofa and had a glass of iced tea. I was desperate to ask her about the punishment which she had endured, so I was lucky that she gave me an entry. She told me that she thought that I was making so much progress that I should soon be able to perform for an audience. I was flattered, but then concerned and wondered what would happen to me if I offended the audience. She told me it wasn't likely, but since they had agreed a universal code of justice I would have to endure the punishment, as she had. I shivered and asked her what it was like. She told me that being displayed was probably the best part. She watched the audience and registered the desire in their eyes and took it as a compliment. The flogging was painful, but it allowed a good deal of erotic behaviour. Another two slashes and she would have had a climax. She was genuinely grateful for my intervention, which she had enjoyed and which had set her up for being fucked by three passengers and a crew member who had lusted after her. By the time that started she was desperate to follow up her orgasms by being penetrated and it seemed to her it didn't much matter who did it. With her head flung back and her breasts pushed forward and her legs apart there was nothing she could do or wanted to do. She just wanted to be fucked and then thrashed again, but no one made use of the whip that was hanging from a hook on the mast.

During this conversation I was becoming distinctly hot and sticky between my thighs and the thought of going through what Miria had suffered made my breathing become rapid and shallow. Miria at once recognised the symptoms and told me that I would have to be careful to make my wrongdoing convincing. We put our heads together and began to plan.

Tonight is going to be the fancy dress dance, easy to organise, the musicians are available whenever needed and if the first time was anything to go by, the choice of costumes is enormous and the wardrobe mistress is an amazing seamstress. I will tell you about it tomorrow.

Keep thinking of me as I do of you. All my love

Laura

Dear John,

I am glad that you are going to Charlie's for the weekend. I wonder who else will be present? Charlie likes a full house with plenty of action. Be careful not to fall for his sister. Her husband has some very big friends who are keen on preserving her virtue, despite her desire to the contrary. Just in case there is any doubt, I give you every encouragement to enjoy yourself as much as you can. As you will soon see, it would be hypocritical of me to deny you any pleasure.

I went to the wardrobe mistress very shortly after she

opened for business. There was no one else there at the time and I had her whole attention. I was wearing my green bikini with a pair of very abbreviated shorts. I think that she is well versed in weighing up what sort of person she is dealing with and what would suit them best. She told me that the green wardrobe was used early in the voyage to give people a chance to wear fairly conventional evening clothes. I had missed the yellow wardrobe, but the red wardrobe was intended to be for those who wished to reveal rather than conceal. I had little idea what she meant, but she picked out three quite different outfits for me. In the end I settled for the dress which covered most of the front of me from neck to ankle, and which was made of dark red chiffon. The top tied over one shoulder and the dress was almost completely backless. The wardrobe mistress made several adjustments to this part of the dress until she was satisfied and invited me to look in the cheval mirror.

The top was now designed to show off almost the whole of my left breast and to be cinched in at the waist with a matching belt. The back was cut so that the fixing at the shoulder led to a narrow band of material which ended below the level of my hips. There was no doubt that I was about to reveal two interesting cleavages. I looked a bit askance, but she assured me that there were some much more revealing outfits which would be worn at the dance. The skirt was in a number of panels, all hanging from the waist and only slightly overlapping. To hold them straight they had small weights in the hem at ankle level. I tried walking about in the outfit and noticed that the panels opened to reveal my legs and even the lower part of my belly. Oddly enough I felt quite excited by the prospect of appearing at the dance in this dress, even though I lacked a partner. As luck would have it I had brought some high-heeled sandals with me which matched the chiffon.

I took the dress off and took it with me in search of Miria. I had forgotten to ask her if she had a partner, but when I did she told me that she was going with Piers, the officer who had superintended her punishment and that she had thought that if I was on my own, perhaps I'd like to meet the second in command, Henry. I was surprised and waited to see what Henry was like. She took me to his cabin and introduced me. He was much younger than I had expected and very good looking in a Greek God sort of way. He was also perfectly charming and gentlemanly and I looked forward to having a partner whom all the other women would envy.

I put on my dress and decided to wear a thong underneath it. I was deciding which one when there was a knock on the door and Miria was standing there in the dress she had chosen for the evening. I was amazed to say the least, and pulled her into my cabin and shut the door. I expressed my amazement, but Miria did no more than laugh. She told me that what she was wearing was quite conventional compared with some of the others. I examined her dress, which was composed quite largely of leather straps each of which had a press stud to join it to the next one. There was a strap which went round the back of her neck and hung down to two straps which divided over her breasts and did nothing to conceal her nipples. These two straps on each side were attached to another strap which went right round her and fitted just under her breasts. In the middle of this strap were two straps about three centimetres wide and fifteen centimetres apart which were joined by a press stud below her navel and crossed over, being drawn between her thighs and up her buttocks until they met the breast band, to which they were attached. In my ignorance I supposed that they were intended to hide her navel and her sex. They certainly weren't doing a very good job with the latter. I told her I was looking for a thong to wear with my dress and she laughed and told me that was not at all a good idea. It would spoil the line of the skirt, and in any event why attempt to cover what was intended to be on view.

She gave me some good advice which was that to ensure a good fit I should wet at least the top half of the dress. I thought I would take her advice and went into the bathroom. I now know why wet T shirts are so popular with men. The material clung to my skin and became almost totally transparent. I tried to dry it off with my hairdryer, but Miria quickly intervened and told me it was just right as I had it.

We went up to the dance floor to meet our partners. They were waiting for us by the door. Piers was wearing a wrestler's outfit which directed eyes, well, my eyes, to his crotch which bulged under the shiny satin. Henry was dressed as a warrior in a breastplate and what seemed to be a leather jock strap. As he took my arm I saw that the top of this garment was open and that nestling within was a flaccid snake of considerable size. As far as I could see there would be no room in his pouch to contain an erection. I decided at once that I must try to seduce him on the dance floor. We went to a table where there was a selection of drinks and watched the other people who had already arrived and those who were just coming in. In almost every case the women were showing off their breasts and buttocks, and not a few their cunts as well. The men were only slightly less brazen, with much attention being given to their crotch areas. There were loosely tied posing pouches and leather items just about held in place with press studs. The variety was endless, even if the theme was similar. The Master at Arms made his appearance dressed as a medieval executioner in an undersized leather apron hanging from a cord round his waist and a mask covering half his face. From his waist band hung the cat o' nine tails which he had used on Miria. Seeing him made me shiver.

Dancing soon commenced and I was caught up in Henry's arms. I pressed myself as hard as I could against him and made particularly sure that my breasts were touching his chest, something which you told me you much enjoyed. I was happy to feel that there was a distinct stirring within his pouch. Miria was standing almost still with her arms round Piers' neck, all of her in contact with his body. She winked at me and pulled slightly away from him and I was delighted to see that the wrestling pants were split into panels and that from one of these splits reared a splendid erection. She very soon closed the gap between them and moved her hips in time to the music. It could only be a matter of time, I thought.

Henry was holding me close to him and I transferred my hold on him so that my right wrist was at his neck whilst my left arm fell free. The lights were dimmed and round us I became aware of hands straying into what passed for clothing and a number of gasps and what sounded like giggles. For a moment I moved away from Henry and slipped my hand between us. My fingers found the top of his leather pouch and the trapped snake. In a moment I had shifted it from its bent position and it sprang into rigid life in my hand, its helmet several centimetres clear of the top of the pouch. I removed my fingers and imitated Miria's dancing pose. Henry pressed himself against me. I was fearful that he would find a way between the panels of my skirt and penetrate me, so I pre-empted this possibility by pulling away from him a little way and returning my hand to his cock. I saw his eyes close as I fingered it and then gave it an experimental tug. He took one arm from my waist and pulled at the gaping part of the top of my dress, wholly uncovering my breast. His fingers were at my nipple in a moment and I revelled in the sparks he was generating. I felt myself go hot and soft between my legs, and gave his cock a few more tugs. I knew that I wanted to be penetrated, but I remembered you.

Near us was a couple who I could dimly make out in the limited light. I realised that she was almost kneeling in front of her partner. I thought this was a very odd position for dancing until I realised what she was up to. As it seemed to be a dance where anything went I decided to see if I could give it a go. I pulled Henry's leather pouch down until his cock and balls were totally exposed. I am a great deal shorter than Henry so I didn't have to bend very far to kiss the tip of his cock. I was delighted to find that it was just slightly sticky and as I licked my lips I enjoyed the taste of something salty and sweet. I'd noticed just what a substantial thing this was that I was trying to get my fingers round and I wondered if it was too big to go in my mouth. I opened my jaws as far as I could and sank my head onto his shaft. I felt it press against my tongue and then his hands were on the back of my head and he was pressing me down further. I had learned from Alison how to pour a pint of beer down my throat without stopping and this ability came in very useful as I felt his cock press against the back of my throat. Even then I hadn't got the whole of it in my mouth and I tried to encircle the lower part with my fingers whilst cupping his balls in my left hand. I tried to nod up and down with my head, but the impact against the back of my throat was more than I could bear. I gently closed my teeth and held him captive whilst using my tongue as far as I could to lick round the shaft in my mouth. I withdrew my head a couple of inches which gave me more opportunity to tug at him with my fingers. I worked him up and down as fast as I could and squeezed his balls with just enough pressure to make him very slightly fearful. I tugged ten, twenty, thirty times and then I felt his balls move of their own accord in my hand. I knew that I was about to be on the receiving end of his fountain and withdrew my head a little more so that he could come in my mouth and I could taste and swallow. I hadn't long to wait and suddenly there was a spurt from his cock which hit the back of my mouth and which I immediately swallowed. He began to spurt into me in real earnest and I was hard put to tug and swallow without wasting any of the precious fluid. The taste was stronger than his pre-come had been, and I enjoyed every moment. I gave him a final lick and pulled up his pouch. His cock was still quite erect, and we danced on, just moving our bodies against one another.

As the set came to an end the lights were turned up slightly and I moved to go back to the table. He walked close behind me trying to conceal the prominent erection which I had generated for him. He swiftly slid into a chair which he drew up to the table. Miria and Piers appeared, Piers having managed to tuck himself into his shorts. We drank more alcohol and indulged in some fairly bitchy discussion about other dancers, some of whom had not left the dance floor and seemed, quite literally, joined at the crotch. At that point an athletic looking young man appeared and whispered in Henry's ear. Henry looked at me with some signs of regret and told me that there was a message for him and that he had to be present on the bridge for a while. I was disappointed, but less so when I realised that the young man in the gold G-string was to take over as my partner. He asked if I would like to see the stars and I looked at Miria, who nodded, and we went up on deck. It was a wonderfully warm night and we walked round the deck in the dark. He put his arm round me and fondled my breast under the chiffon.

As we got to what they call amidships he suddenly pulled me away from the rail and towards the middle of the ship. He told me he had a surprise for me. I thought that if this was what I thought it was I should take his balls in my hand and squeeze very hard. If only you and I weren't together I would have loved him to bend me over the rail and fuck me senseless. As it was I was on my guard with him, but it was not him I had to be concerned about. In the dim light I suddenly saw Miria, Piers, Henry and the Master at Arms. In a moment they had stripped me, put a ball gag in my mouth and had attached me to the net on which Miria had suffered. They made a number of appreciative remarks about the narrowness of my waist and the swell of my buttocks. One of them ran his hand over my back and then Piers spoke to me. He told me that I had been brought before this select gathering, to be stripped naked and to be punished for no better reason than that I was the only woman on the ship who had not been penetrated during the voyage. He told me it would be a test of my fortitude. I looked over my shoulder and saw the Master at Arms off to my left. He was swinging the cat and drawing the thongs through his fingers.

I turned back to the net, pressing myself against the rough ropes in the hope that they would act as a counter to the pain I knew that I was destined to endure. I heard the swish of the whip as it whistled through the still air and then I felt the crack of the tails against my bottom. I saw stars and for a moment stopped breathing. I could not scream, but I moaned and shook myself to try to dissipate the burning sensation which followed the first blinding pain of the whip. I drew as much air into my lungs as I could and held my body taut. There was another swish and another torrent of pain. I threw my head back and looked up the mast which was surmounted by a light which shone among the stars. I leaned away from the net as far as I could only to be thrust against it by the third slash which crossed my back and burnt tracks on my skin. Involuntary tears ran down my cheeks and I tried to move the whole of my body, but to little effect.

There was another lengthy pause and then my hands and legs were unclipped and I was carefully turned round to face the group who were tormenting me. I was reattached to the net, now facing outwards. Piers ran his hand over my belly and then grasped my right breast. He told me that it was just about as beautiful as any he had ever seen, and that I should be less of a tease. I shook under his touch, but when I looked at Miria I saw that she was licking her lips in a way that made me think that she was enjoying my pain and would like to make it worse. All five of them spent some time admiring my naked body. The Master at Arms fingered my sex and I felt a jolt of electricity fire through my belly. His big fingers parted my labia and he thrust two of them inside me whilst turning his hand so that he was able to press on my clitoris with his thumb.

The effect was devastating. I felt the muscles of my belly contract and go into a spasm. I felt an unleashing of something within me which rose rapidly from between my thighs, boiled in my vagina and spread like a fire through my belly and up into my chest. I knew that in a moment it would pulse into my brain and I would have a devastating climax. The Master at Arms was a clever executioner, and having got me virtually to the point of no return he stepped back from me and the others pressed my breasts and stroked my thighs and belly, just to keep me on the boil, but not enough to allow me to boil over.

The group stepped back and I saw that I was to be whipped again. There was nothing I could do about this since I was tied and gagged, but I was not as closely drawn to the net as when I faced it and I could move my body more. The first slash took me across the waist with a couple of strands finding their way to the lower curve of my breast. I gasped and shook myself, which the group seemed to find very agreeable. There was a long pause in which I moved about as much as I could. I began to feel some satisfaction at being viewed, naked, by the five of them. It made my breasts become heavy and my nipples become even more erect. I knew that I was wet between my thighs, but the end of the touching had let me cool down a little. Still, I had my new destiny as a happy exhibitionist and despite the pain I enjoyed the bitter kiss of the whip. After the first agonizing strike, heat travelled through my body and I knew that I wanted to give myself to the stinging thongs as I would to a lover who was stirring me.

I had begun to relax, when a sudden slash across my belly made me jerk forward as far as I could. Before I could recover I received another in the same place and I thrust my body back against the ropes and then forward with my hips tilted to expose myself to the next blow. This soon came and was a devastating cut between my legs and up towards my cunt. The pain was all-consuming, but the pain and the pressure brought me from simply enjoying being displayed, to a sudden renewal of the heat and throbbing in my belly that rose inexorably up into my chest and made my breasts hard and stiff. It then took my throat so that breathing was almost impossible and made my sight grow dim and my mind no more than a wellhead of desire. For a long moment I hung in my bonds almost as if I had been rendered unconscious and then I felt a rush of energy as the throbbing quietened a little and the heat in my vagina increased. My belly contracted in a hard knot and then everything relaxed and I began to gush from between my thighs in a spectacular fountain which amazed the onlookers as much as it did me. Just as this began, Henry pulled the gag from my mouth and I heard myself howl like a wolf in a forest. The Master at Arms waited until I ran dry and became quiet and then gestured Miria to come to my side. He released my ankles and then my wrists and I began to buckle at the knees. Miria held me against herself, stroked my hair and my face and whispered gentle words in my ears.

In a minute I had come round and stood before the group, who kissed me and hugged me and told me how beautiful I was and how well I had gone along with being stripped and whipped. I must say I felt wonderful and I approached the Master at Arms, put my arms round his powerful neck and kissed him. Drawing away I thanked him and then all of them for giving me the most wonderful orgasm of my life. To my surprise Henry told me that I should be thanking Miria who had arranged it all for me so that I could find if this was what I liked or not. It had been a most successful experiment and I hugged Miria and kissed her several times.

The men left the scene and Miria took me by a crew companionway back to my cabin where I was able to wash my face and put the dress back on, since she assured me the men would be awaiting our return. I fixed my hair and put on new makeup and very shortly found myself back in the darkened dance room. Miria led me to our table and Henry and Piers politely stood up to greet us. Wine flowed, I danced with Henry and softened his snake with my hand, there was more wine and I knew that I needed to go to bed. Before I went Miria asked me how it was that I was on this cruise. I told her that you had given me the cruise as a birthday present. I was surprised when she asked me if you had told me that I would be changed by it, since you had, and at some length. In which case, she suggested that you must wish me to take advantage of everything that was available and have as many experiences as I could. I explained that I felt I had to keep myself just for you, but she suggested that I should ask you if I might yield to my desire to be screwed. I thought that was pretty unlikely. She asked me if I had ever been seen naked by a group of people before, or if I had ever been whipped. She knew the answer was no, but she pointed out that you must have known that something like that was very likely on this particular cruise and perhaps you wanted me to have all the experiences that you might like to share with me. Was she right?

I must say his has all been a night to remember and I hope that you have enjoyed yourself just as much at Charlie's. Do let me know.

Yours, anxious to surrender

Laura

Dear John,

Now I understand why you were so bothered about me in an earlier letter. I read yours with growing disbelief and considerable jealousy. You certainly seem to have taken advantage of everything that was available at Charlie's. I hate that Sylvia Armstrong for seducing you, or was it you who seduced her? I can see her perfectly, sitting on a swing with her billowing skirts drawn up to her waist and swinging backwards and forwards teasing you like anything. I am so glad that you hauled her off the swing and smacked her bottom hard and often. However, I was less glad when I read that later on she sat on your lap facing you and that you not only made her come, but screwed her. When I read that I was furious, but on turning the page I see that I have carte blanche to do what I want and fully enjoy every available pleasure. It is too long since I had you between my thighs. I will tell you what it feels like to have someone else where you should be.

I am so glad that you approved of the punishment I was given during the dance. Now I don't have to be so withdrawn I shall endeavour to have as much fun as you have been having, but most of all I shall look forward to coming home and putting these new skills to work for both of us.

This evening has been the fashion show. I had no idea what to wear and, as usual, went to see Miria to get her advice. She suggested that my dangerous bikini would be a hit in the swimwear class, but I pointed out that everyone had already seen that. She asked me if I thought I could try the 'Daring' class and in a fit of enthusiasm, I told her that I would, but it would have to be outrageous. Miria said she had a dress that she was sure I would like and that I could wear it if I wished. I asked what she would wear and she told me that she had a number of dresses at her disposal. Miria opened her wardrobe and started parting dresses on a long brass pole. She extracted a pale grey, long-sleeved dress and laid it on her bed. I can honestly say that I had never seen anything like it. I held it up by the shoulders and it was possible to see right through it. This was because the designer had made it up from the finest silk threads woven in a pattern of spiders' webs.

Miria suggested that I might like to try it on. I quickly discarded my clothes and held the delicate material before me. This had to be the most amazing creation. I rolled up the skirt and started to put it over my head, finding the arm holes with some difficulty. Miria helped me to pull it on to my shoulders and then she smoothed the material over my breasts. Whatever had been added to the silk had made it stretchable and thus each of my breasts was separately covered, and yet at the same time, revealed. Miria continued fitting me into the dress, pulling it smooth over my ribs and then ensuring that every line of my hips, thighs and buttocks was revealed in the skin-tight material. I looked in her big mirror and as I turned I was convinced that my nipples were pressing out between the filaments of the cobwebs. It seemed to me that the dress had done what I thought, given female anatomy, was impossible and had moulded itself across my hips and belly and was clinging to my mons and showing my furled cleft. Below my pussy it clung to my thighs and finished at my ankles. The stretchiness of the fabric allowed me to walk, but I would not have been able to move any faster than that.

Miria produced a pair of sandals with incredibly high heels which emphasised my pussy by tilting my pelvis. She said the dress was a perfect fit and suited my figure. I was so taken by its effect that I asked if I could buy it from her, but she said it was not hers to part with and I didn't press her about it. Miria proposed that I should put my hair up in a French pleat and that she would attend to my make up. This was the most elegant dress I had ever worn, and also the most revealing. Miria asked me if I would mind if she matched my dress with another one. From the wardrobe she took another dress constructed of the same incredibly fine filaments as mine, except that this was made in innumerable diamond shapes and was just the same coffee colour as her skin. She put it on, and I helped to fit it to her. This dress was short-sleeved and had a deep décolleté and a matching scoop at the back. Instead of being ankle length, this one came to just above her knees. I stepped back from her to see what the effect might be and gasped. It was almost impossible to see that she was wearing anything at all! I looked twice and it was only the most intense scrutiny which revealed the filaments in the space between her hips and even there it might have been a trick of the light.

She suggested that we should try to be the last two in the queue to go on the improvised cat walk and that I should go on before her and give the audience a thrill with both the elegance and exposure that my dress provided and then she would follow me and see if they enjoyed the brazen approach.

We did just what she suggested. I waited behind the other women, most of who had managed to find dresses which were cut under the breasts and were slit to the waist. At last it was my turn and I stepped out from behind the screen into the unexpectedly bright spotlight. There was something of a gasp at my entry, but it was only after a few steps that I realised that the spot light had made it appear that I was covered in some sort of transparent glitter, and that had if it not been for the skirt below my knees, they would have been convinced that I had dispensed with a dress and just coated myself in stage make-up. As it was I gained a number of approving comments, both with regard to the elegance and effect of my dress and also the figure inside it. I made the turn to walk back and received an unexpected whistle. I thought that my front view was what would entrance the audience, but I must have assets of which I was almost completely unaware. I moved to the side of the podium to watch Miria begin her walk. Her dark hair was plaited and drawn back from her face, emphasising her magnificent eyes and the dark red slash of her sensuous mouth. What I hadn't bargained for was the shimmering of the apparently transparent filaments of her dress. In ordinary light she appeared almost naked, but in the spotlight it was impossible to tell what she was wearing. The only hindrance to seeing her quite naked was the glittering reflection of the dress. She moved very slowly down the catwalk swaying her hips with each step, holding her head up high and smiling at the audience. Her breasts rolled wonderfully, adding to the cascade of light which shone from her. By the time she was halfway down the catwalk the onlookers were applauding, when she turned and the spotlight revealed every curve of her body, there were cries of well-deserved approval. For some reason I suspected that almost everyone present had failed to equate this vision with the belly dancer they had seen cruelly exposed only a few days before.

We were both summoned before the judging panel and were complimented on our wonderful dresses and our figures. I very much enjoyed the admiration but was surprised that both of us were to be given a prize.

This turned out to be an opportunity to have what they described as a flight in the dark sea. I was asked to put on a swimming costume and come up on deck in ten minutes. Miria went to her cabin whilst I rummaged in my cabinet for a bikini which I hadn't yet worn. I came up with that little black number which has adjustable breast covers and a thong which only just hides my pussy. Miria called for me and I saw that she was unexpectedly wearing a very ordinary gingham print bikini. We went up on deck and were surprised to find everyone assembled. Whatever the flight was it was a new one on Miria and, of course, me. We were promptly made to stand up against a soft plastic covered framework and just as when I was punished, we were spread out in an X shape and secured to the frame. Almost at once I felt the whole thing lift, carrying me at first in a standing position and then horizontal, well up into the air. Miria was still on the deck and I could see her looking up at me as I looked down from twenty feet above her. I realised that I was being swung out over the sea beside the yacht which seemed to be putting on speed. Suddenly I dropped towards the water and I was convinced that the rope holding me had broken and that I would be unable to swim or float when I hit the water. Instead I hit the water with my feet and had a sensation like water skiing. My feet touched only half way down the waves, but there was a fair pull, even so. I was beginning to enjoy this remarkable feeling when the framework began to move towards the horizontal and the water began to pull at my calves and then my thighs. This was an erotic sensation, the more so when the water caught the upper part of my thighs and then tugged at my thong as if it was a lover trying to unclothe me. In a moment the thong was as far down my thighs as the waist band would allow and I revelled in the pressure of water rushing against my pussy and pulsing against my labia and tickling my clitoris. The framework changed angle and I found the pressure had moved to my breasts which were enjoying a wonderful massage from the water. As the yacht sped forward the framework moved and rolled, sometimes concentrating the flow on my breasts and sometimes between my thighs. The pressure of the water became intense and I gave up my open legs to the enjoyment of the push and pull of the tide until I realised that I was panting and that the water was being my lover and moving me towards an orgasm. As far as I could I shifted myself to direct the torrent between my thighs and on to my cunt and I was rewarded by a spasm which joined my juices with the sea.

Someone must have been keeping a careful watch on me as I was then hauled up out of the water and swung back on to the deck. The framework became vertical again and I was greeted by some clapping and laughter. As I was released I realised that my bra was round my waist and my thong round my knees. I quickly tried to pull up my thong and my bra at the same time, an action complicated by Henry enfolding me in a huge white towel. I didn't feel cold in the water, but as I began to dry off I shivered, so that the towel was most welcome, as were the large comforting hands of the second in command. We stood together and watched Miria rise in the air, move out as I had done and then be lowered towards the sea. This time the drop was much more rapid and Miria was almost engulfed before she was hauled up again, still vertical and dropped again into the water. The jolt each time was rather like a bungee jump. The framework tilted and Miria was held almost completely horizontal above the waves. Slowly she was lowered into the speeding water and I saw the water pouring over her shoulders and coming up in a stream between her thighs. I hoped that she was enjoying it as much as I did, but at once she was raised again and then dropped into the water. I now saw why she had been wearing a cheap tie-side gingham bikini as her buttocks gleamed as she was raised momentarily out of the water and her breasts had also lost their covering. Miria was cruelly dunked again and then swung back over the deck. Unlike my experience a crew member strapped a belt round her waist, hooked the rope to it and released her from the framework. This time she was hauled up much higher than I had been and then suddenly dropped into the waves. She came up quickly and tobogganed her body along the waves as she was drawn along. She twisted over, taking the hook with her and lay on her back towed along with the rope between her thighs. She gripped it very tightly and spread her arms out beside her. The audience gave a cheer and she found herself raised out of the water, but because the strap had dragged down to her hips she was head down. I never thought that they would drop her into the water from any height head down, but they seemed to be anxious to half drown her, at least. The effect was to turn her the right way up as the belt moved up from her waist to under her breasts. She was hauled up again and dropped feet first into the water. She had taken up a stance like someone doing the splits and kept it up as she hit the waves, a solid jolt of water thrusting between her thighs. I could see by her face that she had achieved a much wanted release, with her head thrown back and her mouth open. At last she was hauled naked out of the water and arrived on deck to be promptly released from the belt and for Piers to enfold her in a towel the equal of mine.

I supposed that this was the end of the evening's entertainment, and certainly the audience drifted away. Piers and Henry led us away to the ship's gym, where Piers double locked the door. Henry told us that after our soaking we should have a comforting massage and that they would do this for us if we wished. We were both enthusiastic and in a moment we were lying face down on massage tables next to each other. I must say I very much looked forward to feeling Henry's strong hands on my body and I assumed that Miria felt the same. I think we were both surprised when we saw that the two men were drawing on latex gloves. They had had no qualms about touching us earlier, so what was all this about?

Henry poured massage oil into his palm and rubbed his hands together. I felt the warmth of his hands on my shoulders and then down my back. The oil smelled of roses and was a great help to soothing my muscles and generally relaxing me. His fingers explored my back muscles, seeming to give each one a pull and then a push, spreading the scented oil over my skin. I began to relax and Henry moved a little lower, kneading my waist and pressing his strong fingers into my sides. I suppose I should have been concerned, but this time, as I thought of you I also thought of Sylvia Armstrong and I just didn't care. He transferred his attentions to my feet and gave them a delicious massage which made me even more relaxed. From my calves he moved to my thighs and I found myself involuntarily opening my legs so that those large fingers could get a good purchase on my thigh muscles.

Henry may well have been an excellent first officer, but I reckoned that he had another career just waiting for him. Who would not want to run their hands over the naked bodies of young women? Come to that, what young woman could resist having Henry's hands run over her, well, certainly not this one. By this time I felt warm, pampered and wholly relaxed. Henry pressed my bottom and I felt my buttocks close together. He drifted a finger between my buttocks and I felt I could do nothing but relax myself even further. Very gently he pressed his finger against my hidden crater and I drew in a breath in response to the unexpected pressure. Then his fingers were between my thighs and he was paying attention to my pussy. For some reason I was unable to resist him and very quickly he had his thumb pressed between my buttocks and his fingers working on my cunt. Henry bent towards me and asked if I would like to turn over. I sensed that I had no decision to make and he put his hand under my hip and started to turn me. When I was on my side he removed both his hands and I lay in a slightly curled up position with my eyes closed. Henry completed the turning process and I lay, slightly untidily, on my back. It didn't seem to matter to me that I was totally exposed and completely vulnerable.

Henry added more oil to his palm and began to massage my legs and shoulders. He asked me if I would like something a bit more stimulating and took my dreamy acquiescence as approval. He poured more oil into his palm, spread it over both his gloved hands and then ran his hands over my breasts, down my chest and belly and pressed his oily fingers into my pussy. I lay still, hoping that this was the beginning of even better things. In one way I was certainly not disappointed. I suddenly felt my breasts become heavy and my nipples become almost painfully erect. I touched my breasts and they felt solid and hot. Agreeable as this was, it was as nothing compared with what was going on between my thighs, where my cunt had developed a life of its own and was pulsing and lubricating without any conscious effort from me. If my cunt had been a crowd it would be appropriate to say that it was in tumult. I had no idea at all how I could have been so rapidly transformed from a relaxed, supine though completely acquiescent body into some sort of furnace desperately in need of having its fire put out. I had very much appreciated Henry's skilful manipulation, but this was really something else.

I began to take deep breaths and rubbed my knees together. I wanted to dip my fingers in my cunt and tweak my breasts, I wanted to climb up Henry's body, sitting with my knees round his waist whilst he penetrated me and I dripped over his belly, squashing myself against him. I wanted to kneel across his chest and finger my clitoris until I dripped and gushed on him and then rock back until I felt him penetrate me so that I could sit, impaled, across his thighs. I wanted strange hands to fondle my body. I wanted to be hung up, naked, in the town square and be tortured by men in leather aprons whilst the general population crowded round to admire my beautiful body and my response to the pain. I wanted anything and everything to happen to me. My desires were boundless; the ache in my body was intolerable. I shook my head, I mumbled incoherent words, my sight became out of focus and my breasts swelled up with nipples so large that they seemed to have at least doubled in size. My belly was knotted into repeated convulsions and my thighs were involuntarily open. In all this I eventually noticed that Henry was standing beside me looking down at my writhings and mewings. Beside him was Piers who was standing back from Miria and also gazing intently. Henry asked me if I was enjoying the sensation but I could do little more than squirm and drip, and as far as I was able to make it clear that he should do something to help me.

In less time than it takes to tell Henry was naked and was rubbing his gloved hands against his erect penis. I didn't need to tell him that I would provide all the lubrication that was necessary, but he rubbed slowly for several seconds. I looked up into his face and watched it become suffused with a dark red. His cock was nodding in an upright position with its head well above his navel. He reached towards me and pulled me up into a sitting position with my bottom virtually on the edge of the end of the table. I at once put my arms round his neck and drew myself towards him, He raised my buttocks from the table, pulled me towards him so that my cunt was squashed against his midriff and then lowered me onto that magnificent spear which I could feel throbbing as it entered me. I pressed my breasts against his chest and put my lips to his mouth. He slowly lowered me onto his shaft until my bottom touched the table and the tip of his cock was pressing against the neck of my womb.

Very slowly he started to pull back from me and I tried to grasp him with the muscles of my vagina. As I did so I realised that I was on fire inside. His dick was as clever as his fingers. At once I began to sweat copiously and I noticed that Henry was also covered in sweat. As he began to press into me again I held on to him with all my strength, hoping that the inferno raging within me might be stilled by his penetration. If there was a way that this could be done, this was not it. Each successive pressure into my belly seemed to stoke my fires even further. I realised that my pussy was full of my own juices, but too tightly plugged to allow them to run out, so that the force of his penetration was accompanied by a sound which resembled a reciprocating pump operating in deep water. My mouth hung open and I began to dribble down my chin. The sweat became even thicker and stickier and our bodies slid together as if every pore was distributing lubricant. As Henry thrust himself into me for the twentieth or thirtieth time, I had a sudden sense of an overpowering reek from our bodies, a mixture of sweat, my juices, Henry's sweat, the massage oil and perhaps the beginnings of his ejaculation.

Henry leaned his hips away from me until only the tip of his erection was in contact with my cunt. A great gout of juices spurted from me and soaked both our thighs. I felt him release my hip with his right hand and in a moment he was rubbing the glans up and down between my labia, penetrating to my clitoris. I thought that the fire in my belly couldn't be more all-consuming, but now I knew I was wrong. A completely new flame began to burn, half within me and half on my skin. It was penetrating and fierce and made me begin to howl. At the end of each howl I drew in a great draught of air and began another howl whilst I lifted myself up so that I could plunge myself down onto the shaft of his erection.

I grasped him even more tightly so that there was virtually no space at any point between our bodies. I could feel my breasts quite hard against his chest and the nipples chafing as I moved up and down. I tried my best to protrude my belly, feeling the rough curly hair of his groin rasping against my slick skin.

It was only then that I realised that there were three other people howling on varying notes and three other sets of gasping. Whatever it was that had set us off, had affected each of us. I heard Piers cry out and envied Miria the sudden flooding of her cunt. I hadn't long to wait before Henry came to his orgasm and more liquids were exchanged and then dripped onto the floor.

To my amazement, Henry showed no signs of becoming flaccid. After a moment in which he managed to step away from me, and I transferred my hands to between my thighs, where I spent some rapid time in frotting my already flaming clitoris, he returned to me and lifted me off the table, dumped me on my feet and turned me to face the table end. I automatically spread my legs and waited for Henry to slake his lust. I hadn't long to wait. I felt his heavy hand on the back of my neck pressing me down towards the table. As he moved closer to me I felt the rigid end of his sticky cock pressing between my buttocks and for a moment feared he might try to penetrate me in my secret place. I was terrified that his huge implement might do me some real damage, but I needn't have worried as he pulled it down to present it at the gates of my vulva and then began again the long slow penetration I so much desired. Bending over like this foreshortened my vagina and it was not long before I felt an inexorable pressure at the neck of my womb. I knew that Henry was by no means fully into me and I had the sense to scream a warning as his hands clasped my breasts to draw me even closer towards him.

Fortunately Henry realised what had happened and withdrew slowly before returning to press himself into me again and again.

Though the fires still seemed to burn with almost unabated fury, and I managed two more shuddering convulsive climaxes, whilst Henry poured his seed into me, I was aware of the beginnings of a quietening in my seemingly uncontrollable urges. I managed to stand up, turn round and hold Henry against me. The look on his face was amazing. He seemed to glow with pride and passion. I wondered what it was all about, though, to be honest this was a thought in a deep corner of my mind; what I really wanted was to be held comfortingly and to be reassured that all that I had done was in accordance with his wishes and had been to his delight. Amidst the turmoil of my emotions and delights I had suddenly wanted to give myself totally to this man, or, come to that, very nearly any man.

I've never had such a thought before. Nor have I ever felt the stimulation that I experienced with Henry. I wanted to love him and worship him. However, he seemed to be more distant than I had ever seen him since our very first encounter when Miria took me to see him. I feared that he was not interested in me as a person, and one who was in thrall to him, but that having given me all this delight and having no doubt enjoyed my willingness he was now anxious to get on with other matters.

I wanted to cling to him, to press my nakedness against him, but he gently but firmly took my arms from round him and slowly pushed me back to the massage table . I felt the hard edge under my buttocks and began to wish that I had never known the delight and torment of this day. But that was foolish because I had enjoyed everything: the display, the fear, the contact of Henry's hands and his penetration. My mind was in a whirl. I could not believe that I had enjoyed it all as much as I had and yet have regrets. I didn't know what to do, but decisions were again taken away from me as suddenly I found Piers standing in front of me. I looked over my shoulder for an instant to find Miria in the same position as I was, but with Henry in front of her.

Piers smiled at me and tore off the surgical gloves. He asked me if I had enjoyed the massage. I told him that it had lit my fires like no other experience I had ever had. (Sorry, John, but we did say that we would be honest with one another.) He has a very friendly, unassuming grin which completely disarmed me. He told me that they had worn the gloves because Venetia had provided them with some balm which was absorbed through the skin and that the massage was enhanced by the strength of this remarkable potion, which was guaranteed, by Venetia anyway, to bring both parties to the limits of their abilities in the battle of love. I suppose that I should have been furious at being used, but I realised that Henry had used it on himself as well as me, and that I would do my utmost to secure a supply so that you and I might use it.

Piers made no attempt to come closer to me until he gauged my response to what he had told me. Then he reached out a long powerful arm and scooped me up, pressing me against himself and caressing my face and neck with his free hand. He is an expert in mouth to mouth contact, and come to that everywhere else that is available to two naked people. I realised that I was shivering in his arms, but it was most certainly not from being cold. Sensations were welling up in my body from my knees to my throat. I felt a great tension as he stroked my back and bent back my head to kiss me. As I felt his lips on my mouth and his hand on my breast I felt the heat gathering between my thighs. This should not be possible, given the attention I had enjoyed from Henry, but I could not resist concentrating all my attention on the feel of his great rigid shaft pressed against my belly. I felt my insides becoming liquid, and as he continued to hold me in one arm, press his lips to my mouth and then he slipped his free hand between my thighs I knew, even before his fingers opened me and he pressed against my clitoris, that I was about to drip. I did more than that. I positively gushed into his hand and against his thighs. He slipped his forearm under my buttocks and hoisted me up as if I was a doll. I could look over his shoulder whilst I hung on with my arms round his neck and my legs encircling his waist and everything that was vulnerable available to his hands and his shaft.

I arched my body outwards so that he could reach my breasts. His big strong hands were soon cupping each of my breasts and his fingers were tweaking my nipples, pulling them outwards until they were as long and hard as they had been for Henry. He enjoyed this almost as much as I did. I drew myself straight against him and then loosened my legs so that I began to slide down his body. He held me with one hand on my buttocks, a probing finger pressed against my nether orifice. I sensed that I was close to the tip of his shaft and I moved so that I could be sure that it contacted the open lips of my sex. I began to feel his cock slide into me. It seemed to keep penetrating me until I thought it would make me cough, I certainly had trouble swallowing.

When at last his shaft had penetrated me until there was nowhere else for him to go, he gripped each of my buttocks in a hand and began to lift me up on his cock, almost to the point of losing him out of my vagina, but not quite. Each upward thrust was accompanied by a slow fall onto the rigid shaft. I gasped as the tip of his cock struck the opening to my womb. I gasped and then I began, again, to have that sensation of pressure and tension and my muscles bunched on my belly and there was a throb between my thighs which mounted up my body. I had been prepared to give myself to almost any man who showed interest. I was so glad that it was Piers who steadily submitted me to this pattern of penetration and release. I howled in ecstasy and tried to crush him with my arms and legs. It was clear to me that he had not yet achieved his climax, so I locked my legs to his hips and began to thrust myself up and down as hard as I could. The principal effect of this was to renew my passion, so that while he continued to lift me and let me fall, I cried out and moaned as my juices wetted his thighs and my orgasm took over my body and mind.

I could hardly manage any further physical activity. Piers sensed that I had pushed myself beyond the limit and moved me back to the table. I felt the pressure of the edge on the backs of my thighs, and still connected to him I began to release my arms from his neck and curled backwards so that I lay on my back on the table, with my legs wide open and dangling down. Piers recommenced his thrust inside me as my head fell over the further edge of the table. This was an entirely new experience for me. I could not see the man who was penetrating me and I could feel no more than the pressure of his thighs against the inside of mine and the irresistible thrust and withdrawal of his shaft deep into my belly. I gave myself up to being violated with no attempt to do anything but prepare myself for a last climax. Even then I didn't care if I was unable to reach an orgasm. I just wanted him to go on pushing into me for as long as he could. I became almost totally dissociated from reality as the rhythmic pressures increased and decreased. I saw in my mind's eye just the tops of the thighs and the muscular lower part of a man's belly moving backwards and forwards with an occasional glimpse of the long dark shaft on the outward stroke. I was mesmerised and even though I was filled with passion I think I must have lost consciousness for a while. I came to as Piers shot a great pool of jism into me and howled with the delight of his release. He pulled at my arms and I drew my lolling head upwards with my body. He held me close and kissed me again and again. I felt my head fall back against his arm, and the next thing I knew I was sitting on a plastic stool in the shower with warm water cascading over Piers and myself. We spent the night in bed together, but he was gone to his duties before I awoke.

Dear John,

I am sorry that you were cross that you hadn't heard from me the day before yesterday, but that letter took me a long time to put together and there's one characteristic of this cruise that you might have not have taken into account and that is that there is always something going on. I have become part of the group so that it is going on with me as well as them.

Sitting in the sun with my laptop yesterday occupied a lot of my time, especially as I felt I needed to recover from the exertions of the previous day. This will, I think, be quite short as last night was the Poker night. We all sat at tables of four and played five card draw. At the first time round I was with Venetia and a 'married' couple called Charles and Marilyn. He was about fifty five and she was somewhere in her late twenties. I'm not a wonderful card player, as you know, but I was very much better than the couple, though Venetia was a powerful adversary. It didn't take long to get Charles's shirt off his back and Marilyn was soon down to bra and pants. A couple of hands later and they were naked. She has an amazing figure with a tiny waist and large breasts. The way she got out of her clothes made me think that she was well accustomed to undressing in public.

The rule seemed to be that whoever still had clothes moved on to a table with other people who were dressed, whilst the naked ones lolled on settees looking at the players and each other. Once there were a number of people on the settees the lighting was concentrated on the tables so that there should be no distractions for players or audience. You can imagine that the audience might have lost interest in the play except that it was occasionally an opportunity to see a fellow passenger quite without clothes-not always a pretty sight and often hilarious.

We joined Piers and a woman I hadn't spoken to before, called Andrea. She is about fifty but looks strong and well-toned. Piers had lost both his shoes. We played the first deal and I had a good hand. I discarded one card and ended up with two pairs and an ace. The others discarded more cards than I had so I thought I was in a strong position. I bet 10 counters - the loss of twenty means an item of clothing to be removed - Venetia raised me to twenty, Andrea threw in her cards and Piers asked to see Venetia, so I followed suit. Venetia had a full house, so I lost a slipper and Piers had four Kings and a three, so he was down to one sock.

In the second game I was lucky enough to get together a full house on the first deal. Eventually the betting got to forty with a good deal of competition to see who would be seen. This time it was Andrea. She had four Aces and a King. Piers threw in his hand and Venetia turned her cards over to reveal a run. I threw in my cards so they wouldn't know if I had been bluffing or not. I lost my other slipper and my skirt. Piers was down to his trousers.

I thought Andrea had escaped unscathed in her previous games, but she was now down to her bra and pants. The third game was for just twenty.

Venetia seemed to have the luck of the devil in terms of the fall of the cards. So far she had managed to keep herself fully-clothed. The small bet could mean anything. What it did mean was that I was the one in bra and pants, Andrea sacrificed her bra and revealed a pair of small but exquisite breasts, Piers sat in his thong, and Venetia looked smug. The next hand would be the last one. Venetia started at twenty. We all decided to see her. Much to her discomfort her hand wasn't as strong as Piers' and Venetia discarded one of her sandals. Andrea was naked and I was down to my G string. Andrea went to sit on the settee and we were joined by Henry who still wore his trousers. The first hand resulted in Piers and myself being stripped and Henry being reduced to his pants. We went towards the settee as Henry and Venetia went to join a table with a quite well-dressed couple on it. As they got up Henry uttered a loud cry. We turned to see him standing with his hand above his head and a couple of court cards in it. Apparently Venetia had dropped them as she got up. Henry quickly shuffled through the pack and found it had fifty two cards. Venetia had been very good at her sleight of hand. I had suspected nothing. She retrieved her sandal and was led away from the tables.

The eventual winner was a smartly-dressed character who was the image of a Western film gambler. He submitted to a search at the end, but it was apparent that his black suit had no pockets! Clever, or what? Meanwhile, I had had a chance to get together with Miria and Andrea. Tonight is the Cabaret night and we cooked up a little act between us.

I had just come out of the shower when there was a

knock on my cabin door. There was Henry, who told me that he was very sorry that he had, according to the rules, given way to Piers, but that he hoped that I wouldn't be offended if we had a little time together. Henry is a hunk. He's also very well equipped and happily able to make me feel very good. I suggested that it would be nice to relax and turned down the sheet on his side of the bed. I don't think I've ever seen a man who could go from fully dressed to naked in such a short time. We got into bed together and discussed the evening's events. I asked what would happen to Venetia. Henry thought that she would be seriously punished for cheating at cards. The arrangements would be similar to Miria's. With that we dismissed Venetia from our minds and concentrated on our own affairs. I was asleep when Henry left me, though in the morning I could still feel the satisfied smile on my face.

I do hope you are having as enjoyable a time as I am.

All my love

Laura

Dear John,

I see that my hope in my last letter has been realised. I was going to upbraid you for two in a bed until I remembered Henry and Piers. I am glad that your cousins like to keep it in the family, but I thought that one was engaged and the other married. I've probably got it wrong. I thought I was pretty adventurous since I came on this cruise, but you seem to be exploring 'avenues' which I've not yet considered. I do hope your bizarre interests will continue when I get home. Like you I find that I am affectionate towards both Henry and Piers but that love doesn't seem to enter the equation. I could more readily love the executioner. I'll tell you about his latest exploit with Venetia.

I quite like Venetia, but I am also well aware that she is a snotty, pushy cow who seems to think that everyone else is her inferior and that we had better do what she wants us to. She has had considerable influence on what goes on during this cruise, but I rather think that she hasn't made many friends. I suppose that I was flattered that she even took the trouble to speak to me, and having done so she sort of took me under her wing a bit. I much prefer Miria, but then we are more of an age and social disposition and we share an interest which you will probably already have guessed, except it isn't Piers or Henry.

We all gathered before the mast at ten o'clock and spot on time the usual suspects appeared. I must say the Master at Arms looked even more impressive than the last time I saw him. He has a chest like a barrel and muscles everywhere in abundance. His face is adorned with a strongly-grown beard above which his eyes glitter like stars in a forest. I fear I was less attentive to the rest of the people than I should have been as I visualised him going down on me and his huge shoulders between my knees and his beard grazing my thighs as he licked and sucked. I pulled myself together as Henry read out the charge against Venetia and the decision of the passengers at the meeting that she chaired that everyone should be treated alike. I felt a presence beside me and found Miria holding my hand as we stood and waited for the preliminaries to be over.

Venetia had her hair twisted up behind her head which revealed a delicate and striking profile. She wore no make up and her slender figure was encased in the same shapeless tunic that Miria had worn. Venetia had been found guilty of the most unladylike and despicable crime of cheating at cards. She had not denied the charge and it was now time for her to be punished. The Captain had decreed that this should be a hard punishment and the Master at Arms had been given his instructions. Henry asked if Venetia had anything to say. She looked back at him and said that she was sorry, but that she did not want to take off her clothes in public and her only recourse was to make sure that she would win.

Venetia seemed to be the only woman on board who was unwilling to remove most, if not all of her clothes and I wondered why, if it was true, she was so modest in an environment where modesty was generally ignored. She stood straight and did not flinch when Henry told her what had been ordered. The Master at Arms stepped forward and pulled away the fastenings at her shoulders. The tunic slipped down her body which was turned away from us. There was a gasp from the audience as her buttocks were revealed, covered in an obscene tattoo, depicting a huge slavering dog reared up on its hind legs and fucking a woman who was lying back with her legs open and her arms raised towards it. I was not at all surprised that she was shy about revealing this piece of art which hardly fitted in with her normally upper crust pretensions. Miria gripped me very hard and whispered in my ear. I failed to take in what she said as Venetia was being attached to the net.

She is quite a tall woman and slender almost to the point of emaciation. I could count her ribs even before most of her weight was taken by her wrists. In her case her slenderness was accompanied by a very visible muscular development. Her skin looked like an anatomical drawing with muscles and tendons displayed in her arms, legs and back. It was all the more surprising that her buttocks were well-rounded and prominent. As she hung in the net I could see that she was shivering. This had nothing to do with the cold as the morning temperature was already over 30 degrees. I supposed that she was fearful at what was to come. Given what the Master at Arms was preparing for her she had every reason to be.

Henry gave the order to begin and the Master at Arms stepped forward, flexing the muscles in his arms and shoulders. Venetia hung in her bonds displaying her muscles and her buttock art. The Master at Arms drew back the broad thick leather and then slashed it across Venetia's shoulders. She shook her body in response and sinews stretched and danced, drawing muscles into tight knots. She uttered a heavy outflow of breath and I saw her ribs expand as she tensed herself for the next blow. This was not long in coming. The switch caught her across the middle of her back, the edges leaving a parallel track of white marks . She produced a cross between a groan and a cough and shifted herself as much as she could. It was then that I noticed that when she moved her buttocks rolled against each other and the illustration seemed to come to obscene life. The third heavy blow which landed on Venetia's rolling buttocks and this time she let out a howl and drew her head back between her outspread arms.

Despite her slenderness, or perhaps because of it, she presented a most erotic appearance. I was well aware that she was strong and tough, but compared to the Master at Arms who loomed over her, she appeared almost impossibly frail. I was concerned that these heavy blows could do her some real damage, but all that I could see were pink tramlines rapidly developing on her skin. The fourth blow came up in a curve and drove against the top of her thighs and the curve of her buttocks.

Venetia cried out in protest and to relieve the pain. She seemed to want to press herself against the chafing rope as if to punish her front at the same time as her back was receiving so much attention.

I hadn't realised that the Master at Arms was ambidextrous. He crossed over to Venetia's right side and swung the leather to chop her right shoulder. She shook and cried out again, but had little chance to recover before another strike took her below her buttocks which resumed their graphic display of beastliness, or should it be bestiality? The Master at Arms was now intent on striping the whole of her back as fast as he could and a blow to her waist was followed by another across her buttocks and a final strike to her back. Venetia had cried out at each of these blows and she had shaken herself as far as that was possible, but the attack was irresistible and as the Master at Arms stood away from her we could see that there were many crossovers of the tramlines from the right and left and that her body, from the top of her thighs to her shoulders was reddened and had some tiny dots where the blood had come to the surface.

The team was very well practised in arranging the victim for further punishment. So quick were they that they turned and re-attached Venetia in a twinkling. She hung facing us. If the tattoo on her buttocks had been unexpected then her frontal elevation was amazing. Every eye was at once attracted to her belly. On it was depicted a trompe d'oeil coiled snake in the most lifelike colours and as three dimensional as it was possible to get. Its head reached down to the cleft between her thighs and so cleverly was it done that it looked as if the snake had penetrated her. I had never seen anything like it and from the reaction of the audience, neither had they. This time they had attached her to the net with her legs spread further apart but with a bend at the knees. Her arms were much closer above her head. Her face was a mask, revealing nothing of the turmoil which was undoubtedly going on behind it. Her breasts were small but obviously very firm and sharply tipped with pink nipples which stood out from the points of her breasts, seeming to extend them forwards and upwards. Her ribs were all visible and her tiny waist sank into hips whose bones shone whitely through her skin. She was utterly devoid of body hair which made the questing snake very much more visible. With her legs drawn away from each other the lips of her sex were very slightly parted, making the snake's head seem to have pressed its way within her. Her thighs were remarkably slender, but revealed powerful muscles which moulded them into athletic curves. She looked out over us without any sign of recognition that we were admiring her tattoo or her sinewy, toned body.

The Master at Arms had chosen a quite different weapon for his renewed attack on her. It was a slender plaited-leather whip about a metre twenty in length with a knot at its tip It was obviously very pliant and I thought it would wrap itself across and round Venetia's body. The Master at Arms stood to Venetia's right and extended his hand to take her left breast in his fingers. He must have pinched her nipple because she gave an involuntary gasp and tried to jerk away from him. When he removed his hand it was apparent that the nipple was fully erect so he repeated the exercise on her right breast, first cupping the breast in his palm and almost totally obscuring it, and then tweaking her nipple. This time she was ready for him so that she gave no evidence that he had done anything to her, except that when he withdrew his hand her nipple gave away the effect that he had on her. He bent his head to kiss her mouth. She tried to evade the touch of his lips, but in unsuccessfully doing so, she failed to realise that his large hand was poised over her sex and in an instant he had pushed his fingers into her and was using his thumb to massage her between her labia.

He certainly knew what he was doing for she immediately stiffened and then thrust her hips towards him, increasing his penetration of her and making it easier for him to locate that little sheathed button of flesh which contains so many nerve endings directly connected to her pleasure zone. I watched as she began to pull on the straps which bound her wrists and thrust her knees even further apart. Her chest developed a visible flush and her nipples stood out from her breasts in even greater relief. She began to gulp in air and blow it out in long sighs, providing a voiced accompaniment of eerie sound which filled the ears of the audience. The Master at Arms obscured a good deal of her from view whilst he manipulated her sex. He was looking closely into her face and as her howl changed note he stepped back from her and we all saw that her belly was reticulating with the muscles standing out in relief. The snake was moving with the most lifelike action so that its head appeared to be pushing deep into her cunt, whose lips seemed to open and close in rhythm with the muscles of her belly. Thirty seconds after the Master at Arms had disengaged his big fingers from her she twisted and writhed in her bonds and her juices became evident at the underside of her slot and began to drip on the deck.

This was what he had been waiting for and the Master at Arms sliced his whip across her belly so that her orgasm was compounded by a viciously painful cut at a point where muscles were most in tension. She responded by twisting in her bonds and crying out, but this was to be only a preliminary to further strikes on her body. The next was just below her breasts and I watched in wonder as her ribs expanded until it seemed they would burst through her skin. The intake of breath fuelled a shriek, which was repeated as he caught her across her breasts and the end of the whip twisted up into her armpit. Tears were running down her face to match the continuous flow of her juices. Three further strikes caught her across her chest, her waist and the top of her thighs. Her head was now well back between her arms and she was hanging with her body bowed outwards, unable to avoid the burning cuts from the whip and given over to her own arousal. This part of the punishment was brought to an end with three strikes upwards from ground level so that the slender part of the whip caught her between her thighs and her howl became one of agony and despair. She hung almost unmoving, the tears dripping off her chin onto her breasts, and her breathing laboured and stertorous. Her juices continued to flow from her cunt which had decided that it had a life of its own to fulfil.

With her head back and her eyes closed, Venetia was not aware that this part of the punishment was over. Her body was decorated by numerous weals and it sagged on the net with her ankles far apart, but her knees bent outwards to reveal the barbarous art work and every detail of her naked cunt. Henry announced that the formal part of the punishment was over, but that Venetia must hang where she was for two hours and eighteen minutes and that during that time any member of the crew or passengers might do whatever they wished with her, provided she was not damaged and that blood was not drawn.

The Master at Arms looked round at us with a questioning expression on his face. As soon as we worked out what it was he was querying there was clapping and shouts of 'Do it,' and 'Go on.' He seemed happy to abide by the audience's encouragement and stood in front of

Venetia's hanging body, stepped out of his uniform trousers and bent his knees between her legs. In a moment he had engaged himself with her and began to thrust himself inside her until he lifted her clear of the lower bar of the net whilst holding her up with nothing more than the rigidity of his massive cock. He stood unmoving as Venetia drew her head up from where it had fallen back during the whipping and stared at him with wide-open eyes and a mouth which was a perfect O. It was evident that she could not believe that he had been able to transfix her so that she could not move, but she must have felt him pressing against the neck of her womb, which was really the only point of contact between their bodies. Venetia realised that he was about to do something more to her and her face took on an expression of fearful concern. The Master at Arms reached his hands behind her and took a buttock in each of them. Without any seeming effort he lifted her up until the shackles on her ankles prevented any further movement. He held her with just the end of his erection penetrating her and then dropped her on to his shaft, watching the grimace which indicated that he had penetrated as far as was possible into her guts. This performance continued for many minutes until Venetia called out in a despairing wail. The Master at Arms' response was to grip her by the hip bones, force his legs together and start thrusting in and out of her. She cried out, but his thrusting was relentless and with each thrust he shook her entire body, making her breasts bounce and her head nod uncontrollably. She seemed like a rag doll in his massive hands, quite unable to prevent what was happening to her. As his assault proceeded she looked into his face and then, wonder of wonders, she smiled at him and opened her mouth to cry out as he brought her to another climax and he shot his jism deep into her.

He held her close to him and wrapped his massive arms round her. In an unexpected gesture of gentleness and intimacy, he brushed his lips down the side of her face and then touched her mouth lightly with his. For a man of such size and strength, who seemed to represent bitterly painful discipline, this was a most unexpected act, but it was much appreciated by the audience, with renewed applause, and if her expression was anything to go by, by Venetia.

At this point, the Master at Arms detached himself from Venetia. As he began to step back he stroked his hand down her body and in return she pulled in her belly and gushed juices and jism from her sopping cunt. None of the men seemed keen on following the Master at Arms either by enjoying Venetia's body or punishing her further with any of the implements available. One or two of the women went up to Venetia and told her how brave and beautiful she was, but they drifted off very quickly. In the end Miria and I were left alone with Venetia. She was clearly exhausted and her weals were beginning to burn in the powerful sunlight. Miria produced a bottle from her bag and suggested that we should apply a layer of the balm to Venetia's body. Venetia managed to say 'Please,' and we went to work.

One of the interesting things I have learned on this cruise is that people have widely different body textures. Some are like sponges and the mass of their flesh slips through my fingers, others, like Miria, are soft but have an underlay of powerful muscle. In Venetia's case she seemed to be hard and bony. Even her buttocks and her breasts were strong and firm. I found a cloth and a drinking water fountain and washed her face. It was clear that the pull on her wrists and arms, even despite her slight weight, was causing her considerable pain. I told Miria that I was going to risk lowering Venetia's arms and reattaching them to the net. There was no one about and I made the adjustment without it being too obvious. Venetia was now able to lean back against the net and take a lot of weight off her arms. I gave her a drink of water, and then another one. She seemed to revive substantially. I asked her if the whipping had been very painful. She told me that it was utter agony, but that it was accompanied by a strange sensation of release. She had wanted the Master at Arms to hold her in his arms and felt great delight when he had done so. She wanted to give her body to him to do whatever it was that he wanted and he had sensed her desire for him and he had entered into her with power and pain, but with passion, at least on her side.

Once she was irrevocably naked she didn't mind being displayed, in fact she had positively revelled in the gasping surprise of her audience. I gave her some more water and she told us something of her past history when she was employed as part of a troupe of entertainers by a wealthy oil sheikh. It was there that she had learned to wrestle and to be displayed naked for the pleasure of the sheikh's guests. It was there that she had come across the Chinese tattooist who had decorated her body whilst she was under the influence of powerful narcotics. She had continued to serve the sheikh for three more years, during which she had learned to rotate her buttocks so that the figures appeared to be fucking, and to knot up her belly and open the lips of her sex so that the snake was apparently pleasuring and penetrating her.

There was much more, but we stayed with her until Henry and two crew members came to end her punishment. We took her to her cabin, gave her a shower and a douche and used Miria's balm to quieten the weals. We put her in her bed and Miria obtained a light meal for her. She was halfway through it when she became drowsy and her head nodded. We fluffed up her pillows and as her head sank into them she seemed asleep. We removed the remains of the meal and shut her cabin door behind us. In the companionway, Henry was standing with his arms folded. Miria and I looked at each other with concern, but Henry merely thanked us for looking after Venetia and invited us to share his table at lunch.

There is more to tell you, but it will keep to another time.

All my love

Laura.

Dear John,

I know you always had a penchant for girls with red hair, but do be careful. This one sounds like a man-eater and I shouldn't want you to be consumed utterly. This club you went to sounds very interesting. I am not at all sure about drawing cards to pair off. What happens if you really don't fancy the one who falls to you? Still, I suspect that you were all too sozzled to bother. Why don't I like that idea, after all we agreed that we could do whatever we wanted whilst we were apart. Still, a visit to the dungeons does sound rather frightening. However did you manage to volunteer for the rack? I bet it hurt dreadfully. I can't help visualising your naked body stretched out on the table with the ropes tightening and drawing you into tension. I bet you enjoyed the audience watching you and licking their lips. The whole idea made me lick mine, too.

Things have been going on pleasantly enough here. We have had excellent food and pleasant company.

Venetia has become very friendly to both of us. She confided much of her previous life to me and in return I told her of my dark secret longings to be displayed, naked, and to be whipped and fucked before an appreciative audience. She asked me if I had ever had any sort of experience like that and I said that I had quite recent experience, though I didn't enlighten her as to what that was.

Tonight is cabaret night and Miria and I are going to perform as the last act on the bill. There will be quite a few of the audience who will be waiting to see our display. I will tell you what happened tomorrow.

Look out for yourself. Lots of love

Laura.

Dear John,

I have asked Venetia if she knows you. She was very guarded at first and wanted to know why I was interested. I didn't let on that you and I are an item. I told her that you were an acquaintance who worked in the city. She asked me about my boyfriend, so I invented an older, married man, who I was deeply in love with and who had paid for my cruise so that I would be more adept when I returned. She seemed to swallow this and then she told me a lot about you. It was a great deal more than I have ever got to know, which didn't really please me. What's more I was unaware that you were quite so dominant and that you manage to attract a bevy of young women, and apparently some older ones, who wish to come under your spell. From what Venetia told me I can understand your generosity in giving me this cruise. I had much to learn, and perhaps still have. What I don't understand is why you didn't come along as well. From what you tell me you are using your leisure very successfully. I know you haven't forgotten me, but I do hope that you will be pleased to welcome me back. I shall look forward to your account of George and Margaret's Club

Since you are so keen to know, I had better tell you about last night. I spent the day sunbathing and swimming. You would hardly recognise me. This is the deepest tan I've ever had and I have been very crafty, and careful, so that there is really no part of me that is still white or pink. Fortunately Miria has been a great help to me. She doesn't go any darker than she already is, and so I am rather darker now than her Latte coloured skin. This goes rather oddly with blonde hair and blue eyes, but there are people in North West Africa who are similarly coloured, though their features are not at all like mine. I think Miria is the most beautiful woman I have ever seen. I've already told you what she looks like, but it is the feel of her body which is so enchanting. She is not soft or floppy, but she is covered with a wonderful, smooth skin which sets off her svelte body and makes me want to touch and hold her close to me. Until the fashion parade I was unaware what my own body was like, though I thought it was pretty much passable. It was only when I realised that I could wear Miria's clothes that I worked out that we were so similar in size and shape. I am nothing like as fluid in my movements as Miria is, and I'm perhaps a little more obviously muscular, though I suspect that she is stronger than I am.

We have decided to take up where Miria left off last time and was punished for what was seen as self indulgence. Our rehearsal was a full dress affair, if you can call what we were wearing, full dress. I have obtained permission from the entertainments committee to do whatever we wish once we get going on our act. We are allocated only 12 minutes.

The time came and we watched the other acts from the side of the stage. There was a couple who I had hardly noticed before who sang hits from the shows and were really very good. To our amazement, Dr Nicholas appeared and performed several very intricate magic tricks to an entirely professional standard. I was within two metres of him, but I had no idea how he managed to conjure up fire, the image of a couple kissing or a large grey and white cat. I've no doubt that he would have been applauded for anything he did, but the audience gave him a standing ovation, which was well deserved. Following that one of the crew turned out to be an excellent stand up comic and even managed to do an impression of Dr Nicholas complete with a magic trick involving a stuffed owl.

Then it was our turn. The lights were dimmed apart from a couple of spots on the stage. We wore belly dancer's costume of jewels in our hair, a small gauzy yashmak, Loops of beads over our breasts, dangling from our necks and held to our nipples by clips which just served to emphasise their length and erectness. Each of us had a belly button stud, though as neither of us is pierced, these were held in place by wig glue. The skirts hung as low as was possible on our bellies and buttocks, strapped in with Velcro. Miria had produced two skirts I had not seen before. They were of some satin material with numerous slits to the waist band, and with weighted hems. There was something about this material which made it cling to our bodies and yet it was able to fly up if we spun round. Our feet were bare but decorated with stripes of colour and an anklet on each leg.

The music started off quite slowly, which gave us the

opportunity to drift round the stage only half a metre from the audience and shake our breasts and buttocks, apparently much to their enjoyment. As the music increased a little in speed we stamped our feet and shook our bellies. With our hands above our heads this meant that our skirts descended two or three centimetres, which in both our cases gave our onlookers a tantalising glimpse of the beginning of the furrow below our mons. It wasn't at all clear to me how we managed to retain our skirts, but then, women have much more delightful buttocks than men so they probably saved the day for us.

We were each able to engage in a variety of erotic undulations and jiggling of the more luscious parts of our bodies and continued until the music paused momentarily. This was the signal for the belly dance to become more of a striptease, something which I knew several of the men in the audience had requested. We reached to the fastenings of our skirts and pulled them open. I grasped mine in both hands and raised it to breast height, covering the whole of the front of my body. Miria had taught me how to spin without becoming dizzy and we both rotated at increasing speed, still holding our skirts but lower down our bodies. After a dozen or so turns, we stopped and reversed our spin, holding the skirts out before us, first of all with both hands and then, to immediate applause, with one. We swooped our skirts down towards the ground and then up across our bodies and finally, above our heads. The audience had a full view of our naked bodies in motion, but I am sure they were surprised to discover that our lower bellies and between our thighs had been decorated with theatrical glitter. You might have thought that this would conceal our intimate areas, but in fact it enhanced every curve and fold. Suddenly the music stopped and we sank on one knee, facing the audience. There was much applause as the onlookers thought that the performance was finished.

Miria and I walked to opposite sides of the stage and dropped our skirts, took off our yashmaks and removed the clusters of beads from our necks and breasts. The audience remained quite silent as a thick rubber practice mat was unrolled on to the stage. Here we were, having titillated them, now completely naked and about to do they knew not what. We walked to the front of the stage and bowed to the audience and then turned and bowed to each other. We stepped back to the centre of the stage and faced each other. We had carefully rehearsed the sequence of actions, but even so we were both nervous as we looked into each other's eyes.

We each reached out a right hand towards the other's neck, whilst our left hands tried to slip under the other's guard. We moved with deliberation and tried to throw each other by forcing a leg between the other's legs. We became a bit wobbly, but the throw was ineffectual. We made grabs for various parts of each other's bodies, now urged on by shouts from the audience who were about evenly divided in their support for us. In a classic move, Miria dropped to one knee and I fell backwards over it with my waist across her bent thigh and my feet on one side and my head on the other. I grabbed at her arm to pull myself up, but she brought the flat of her hand down with a resounding smack on my taut belly. This effectively drove a good deal of air out of my lungs, and she repeated the smack three times before I was able to roll off her knee on to the floor. I was face up and she immediately sprang on top of me with her hands on my arms and her shins on my legs. The only trouble with this manoeuvre is that there isn't a lot that can follow it unless the grip is broken. I heaved up with all my strength, but she maintained her position. However, we were both hot and sweating and this began to make our bodies slippery. I managed to free one of my legs and kicked out hard with it. In the ensuing melee I managed to reverse our positions so that I was now on top, but I was using my shins to trap her arms and I was pressing down on her knees with my hands.

I suddenly became aware of the noise that the audience was making and looked up. I should have concentrated on Miria, as she managed to free her right arm and as I knelt over her I suddenly felt the dreaded orifice clutch. She had at least two fingers inside my cunt whilst her thumb had penetrated my rear passage and was well past my sphincter. I had no idea what to do as her fingers and thumb tightened their grip on me. I thought that I would try to raise my body, but her elbow was on the mat and her forearm was vertical I pushed back as she increased her grip and I could feel her fingers nearly meeting her thumb in the delicate insides of my holes. I let go of her knees and tried to penetrate her with my fingers, but that meant leaning forward so that she was able to increase the pressure she was exerting. I let out a howl and tried to shake my body so that she would slip out of me, but my effort was quite unsuccessful. I tried reaching back to seize her arm, but a sharp twinge between my thighs warned me that this would be unwise. I sat up and found that she had reached round with her left hand and had grasped my left breast and was pulling it and sinking her nails into it whilst tweaking my nipple. I could deal with this hand, but as I tried to lever it off, there was another sharp increase in the fingers biting me below. I tried to think of some tactic which would free me from the savage grip, but as I tried to sit back on her belly Miria's left hand plunged between my legs and found my open lips. It was a matter of a moment before she had engaged her fingers with my clitoris and had begun rubbing away at it.

In a gesture of abandonment I laced my fingers together behind my head and awaited the inevitable. I half sat with my knees apart as far as they would go, my holes gripped like a vice and adept fingers working on my pleasure bud. My nipples were hard and erect, my breasts felt heavy and full, my pose revealed all that I normally kept hidden and this thought alone was enough to start the fluttering in my belly and the heat boiling up between my thighs. The spotlight was in my eyes, but I became aware that the audience had got out of the chairs and everyone was crowding round to see just what was going on.

The fluttering became a beating and thunder roared in my head. I began to howl, partly with the pain of Miria's grip and partly because I wanted to come and spurt over her. She knew so well how to play my body. Each time I was about to climax she gave a jerk on her inserted fingers and then stopped her work on my clitoris. I thought that I would take over this task, but her grip warned me off. Instead I drew in my breath and cupped my breasts in my palms, working on my nipples with my first fingers and thumbs. Now I knew that whatever Miria did it would not be long before I gained my all-consuming release. This time there was no increase in the bite of her grip and her fingers continued to rub between my labia. The sensation was mind numbing, but not numbing to my feelings. I had no desire but to give myself up to this cruel grip and the increasing pressure on my nub. I pulled and tweaked my nipples and clawed at my breasts, and then I felt it. It was as if a valve had suddenly been turned and the pressure in my belly was released. I could feel the spurts of juice gushing from my open cunt and I cried out in a sudden and overwhelming ecstasy.

Miria removed the hand that gripped me, but continued to manipulate me between my legs as I fell on to all fours. I continued to drip and have ripples of fire reaching up through my belly into my chest. I could hardly hold myself up on my hands and knees, and as Miria withdrew her hands I slid forward to lie between her knees. There was a hubbub from the onlookers. I started to lever myself up and turned towards Miria who was supporting herself on her forearms. There was a puddle of my juices on Miria's belly and some on the practice mat. Miria drew up her knees and sprang to her feet. She stood in front of me as I kneeled and I looked up to see her wonderful belly and breasts. I made out a chant from the audience as Miria looked down at me and smiled. She moved a few centimetres towards me and I obeyed the demand of the voices all round us. I reached up and opened her lightly furled lips. I saw the bright line of pink within them and the slightly darker point where her nub lay. I pressed my forehead against her belly and grasped a buttock in each hand. I tilted my head and pushed out my tongue as far as it would go and stroked it between her smooth sex lips. I was lucky that my very first track between them allowed me to catch her clitoris. I held my tongue as stiffly as possible and licked up and down until I became aware of a slight change in the taste and feel of her, from very slightly acid and just damp to almost sweet and increasingly warm and wet. I changed my position and took her nub between my teeth. I heard her gasp and her body become rigid. Perhaps she thought that I was looking for revenge for the grip she had put on me. Nothing could have been further from the truth. I was desperate to make her come as she had me. I knew that her dark, passionate nature could lend itself to being rapidly stimulated and produce a climax even more devastating than mine. I wanted to be the one to do it and I nibbled and licked until I felt her belly contract and her juices began to drip. She put her hands on my shoulders for a few moments and then started to lean back. I began to lap and nibble with increasing speed and pressure as I held on to her buttocks. Almost at once I was aware that she was leaning the top part of her body away from me and pushing her cunt even deeper into my mouth. I started to lap up her juices as fast as I could, and then she tensed against me and she cried out as she released a stream of juice into my open mouth. I swallowed quickly, but there was far more than I could manage and it streamed down my cheeks and chin and splattered on my breasts and thighs and onto her feet. Her hands were on my shoulders again and I stood up, trailing fingers into her cunt to manipulate her clitoris. I thrust my breasts against hers and gently pressed my lips against her mouth. Her eyes were closed and I was conscious that she was still coming, so I worked harder with my fingers, held her as close as I could and slipped my tongue between her lips and teeth. I felt her give a jerk and the juices increased on their way down her legs and on to the mat. She almost fell on me. I felt her body begin to relax and I caught her under the arms and lowered her and myself into a little tableau on the floor where I cuddled her and kissed her and, at last, she put her arms round me and looked into my face and kissed me long and deep.

The people who were looking at us clapped and cheered until we both managed to rise and bow and then walked off the stage.

Having showered and resumed some more conventional clothes we wondered whether to just lock the cabin door and spend the night together, or to return to the deck and behave as if butter wouldn't melt in our mouths. In the end we decided on a little walk and joined the company in the bar. Almost at once we were plied with drinks and not necessarily welcome attention. However, a middle-aged man came to see us and handed each of us a card. He congratulated us on our performance and invited us to contact him when we returned home. It seems he is a very famous impresario, though how he could put us on the stage I have no idea, but then, I don't have to have any idea.

We were both wilting a little so we settled for the other option and spent a blissful night together.

Please tell me what you have been up to. I am sure that it is much more interesting than my escapades.

I love you very much

Laura.

Dear John,

You are quite wrong. I have not changed into a Lesbian, though I have to tell you that I have never felt so free to experiment with both sexes. What I need here is a loving friend to provide me with comfort and appreciation. I think you should be pleased that my friend is a woman. After all, she doesn't present any sort of threat to our relationship. On the other hand, she is quite beautiful and I have learned to enjoy her body and let her enjoy mine. The whole feeling is different between the two of us from what we have between you and me. I am beginning to know what it is I want, and I need love and affection quite as much as sex. However, none of these in a relationship with a woman is going to produce children, so I think there's a certain aridity about it, but the pleasure is wonderful and I look forward to having many women friends during my life.

There's a small matter of your recent experiences which have made me jealous. Or perhaps just envious of some of the women in your life. I have no idea who Jacqueline is, but your description of her makes me think that you may be in danger of falling in love with her, which would not be good for the relationship that we have. I appreciate her desire for you to be rough with her. You are a big strong man, so that you would have no difficulty playing the part, even if you were attempting to be careful. I should have made some very adverse comments about her desire for you to rip off her clothes and be put over your knee and spanked, preferably with others looking on, if it weren't my own wish for something very similar, but much more elaborate and ritualistic. Personally, I think that being put over a knee, naked or not, is just a bit little girlish; or is that how she is entrapping you? If she is still around when I get home I shall have the greatest pleasure in introducing her to some much more fruity delights.

Tonight there is a party for Dr Nicholas's birthday. I gather that it will be mainly food and drink, both in large quantities. Do tell me more about Jacqueline.

Lots of love

Laura.

Dear John,

I thought that some of my experiences were quite inventive, but yours seem to have gone much further. I do think you should be careful with what you do to Jacqueline. I can see the delight in tying her wrists behind her back, but then dunking her in the hot tub seems a bit risky. As for then turning the heat up slowly when she

194

was unable to get out. Well, no wonder she went lobster colour. She must have endured a terrible pain when you hauled her out and threw her in the cold water. I'm not surprised she didn't scream, she probably was in a total state of shock. Do be careful, I don't want to be called as a character witness at your trial and have to say what a big softy you really are, especially as I don't believe it. If she then let you push yourself into every orifice, I can only think that she is a thorough going masochist, and if that is the case, beware, they're not easy to live with.

  Keep at it

Love

Laura

Dear John,

I intended to write tomorrow, but I just had to tell you about the party. We were anchored off a small island so that everyone on board could be present. A buffet had been laid out on four big tables and I can honestly say that I have never seen anything like it. The chefs had done a wonderful job of preparing hot and cold food, some very plain and traditional and some which was so exotic that I often had difficulty recognising what it was, despite the labels which neatly detailed what each platter contained. I ate until I was full, though each of my portions was tiny, so that I could try as many as possible. I shared a table with Miria, Henry and Piers, who were more selective than I was, but also had much larger portions. Wine of every delicious and singularly intoxicating sort flowed into our glasses. I became both well filled and also rather woozy.

Miria and I had decided that a bit of ethnic dress would be a good idea. Miria wore a flame-coloured sari whilst I managed to get into a skin-tight cheongsam which sported two side slits. I hadn't realised that these were closed half way up my thigh by a Velcro tag until Henry slid his hand on to my knee and I then felt his fingers on the inner face of my thigh. I didn't do anything about it because I thought that the seam would prevent too much of an intrusion, but he levered the Velcro open and the slit made me accessible to my waist. I should have objected, but I found the firm touch of his strong fingers drifting up my thigh, invisible to everyone else, very exciting. I was sitting with my knees pressed together in accordance with the needs of the pencil slim skirt, so that his fingers reached my belly and then stroked down towards my thighs. Being surreptitiously seduced in public is very much of a turn on. I sat back in my chair, opened my knees a little now that one seam was open, and enjoyed his ministrations as he carried on a conversation with Piers on the subject of desirable cruising locations. He was definitely cruising my skin, and I enjoyed every moment of it.

I tried my best to carry on a conversation with Miria and Piers, but every so often I

could not resist a little gasp as Henry's fingers found something delightful to do between

my legs. The band started playing some dreamy, slow melody and Henry suggested that we might have a little dance. I was torn between the prospect of holding him against me and the current delight of his fingers probing under the skirt of my dress. My decision was made for me as he withdrew his hand and began to stand up. He politely stood behind my chair and drew it back as I began to get up. Piers and Miria followed suit and soon we were standing on the dance floor. I was holding on to Henry with my fingers laced round the back of his neck. I pressed my body against his and was very conscious of the stirring at his crotch and the powerful pressure of his erect cock against my belly. I was all for staying on the floor for a couple of tunes and then moving away to either his cabin or mine.

Seemingly out of nowhere I felt Henry start to move away from me and even though I was fairly fuddled I realised that someone else had cut in between us. I didn't have time to be cross or object before I was clasped by none other than Dr Nicholas! I attempted a more formal grasp of my new partner but he gently put my arms up and my hands behind his neck. Curiously, I found this even more agreeable than with Henry, partly because Dr Nicholas is rather shorter, so that I wasn't hanging on to his neck, but just using it to draw our bodies together, and partly because he is a very powerfully-built man and pressing my breasts against his chest was like encountering a solid wall. For some reason this gave me a little quiver which he certainly recognised as he smiled into my face and kissed my cheek.

We stood together swaying gently and moving our feet so slightly that we made no visible progress across the floor. His arms were around my waist with his hands holding me close to him. I began to feel his hands move down the small of my back and then on to my buttocks. He pressed me against his crotch and once more I became aware of his rising interest in me. Within a moment he had managed to find the open slit in my skirt and his hand was on my naked buttock. I found this a strangely reassuring gesture and leaned my head on his shoulder. His hand remained still for a minute or so and then his fingers moved to the cleft in my buttocks. The lights were very dim and I didn't suppose that anyone else was interested in what he was doing to me, since they had pleasures of their own to explore.

Dr Nicholas had long arms as well as strong ones. Having explored the valley of my arse he adjusted his stance very slightly so that the tips of his fingers encountered the extremity of my cunt. I pressed myself even closer against him to ensure that he made no frontal attack on me, but also to ensure that he had better access from the direction from which he was operating. I moved my head and looked up into his face as he pulled my labia apart. My reward for this was the pressure of his lips on my mouth and a pulsing in my belly.

He seemed pleased at the gathering dew between my thighs and kissed me again. He whispered in my ear and withdrew his hand. I couldn't believe that twice in the evening he was going to be responsible for my frustration and I tried to cling on to him as hard as I could.

He smiled down at me and repeated what he had just said. I was more attentive this time and realised that he was inviting me to accompany him on deck. I released my grasp on him and we turned towards the companionway which led up to the deck. As we were about to ascend, he touched my shoulder and asked me if I would rather see his cabin. This was a rare invitation since no one on board that I had spoken to had ever seen inside it apart from his valet who was the most taciturn of men. More than his job was worth, I suspect.

His cabin occupied the full width of the stern of the ship and had en suite facilities of every sort that I could have imagined. It was decorated in an almost Baroque style with much gilding, white paint and Ionic columns. The furniture provided a hint that the cabin could be used for business meetings and also for other purposes. The bathroom was almost four metres square, complete with a large corner bath, a circular free-standing shower, a bidet, two adjacent sinks and matching toilets, and a large hot tub and Jacuzzi. There was a huge mirror on the wall behind the sinks below which was a shelf with every sort of skin pampering lotion that it would be possible to imagine. A pile of clean white towels rested on a unit which blew warm air into them. Nothing that could make for comfort and cleanliness had been forgotten. He stood behind me in the bathroom and pointed to the lighting. He uttered a low whistle and the lights dimmed. I was childishly delighted. I looked into the mirror and was not at all surprised when he took each of my breasts in a big hand and bent his lips to my neck; I couldn't have asked for more. I felt a shudder go through my entire frame as he squeezed and kneaded my breasts beneath their satin covering. I thought that I was about to get lucky, the more so as I could feel his rampant cock pressing between my buttocks. Sex whilst wearing layers of clothing has never appealed to me. I took his hand in mine and traced it down the front of my body and then to the side where I inserted it into the slit in my skirt. His hand rested on my belly and then I felt the steady pressure of his thumb on my navel. This isn't painful, but there is something about it that makes me draw in my breath abruptly and tremble. I leaned back against him and watched in the mirror as his hand billowed the front of my skirt and his fingers reached for my pussy.

I shook under the pressure of his fingers, but he spoke to me again and I got the message at once. He asked me if I agreed and I told him that I did. We left the bathroom and went into the cabin. I turned towards him and bent to the hem of my skirt, drawing it up my body until it was up to my chin and he was able to pull it over my head. Though it was the closest possible fit, it had the advantage of a long zip which made getting into and out of it rather easier. I have come to enjoy the admiration that I see in men's eyes when they can take a good look at my naked body. I turned slowly round so that he could see me from every angle. I knew very well that I had him on a line. He suggested that I might stand for a moment between two of the columns so that he could admire the three sets of curves. I was quite willing. He invited me to raise my arms against the columns and place an ankle against the base of each of them. I was about to receive another surprise at the effectiveness of the technology as I at once found that my wrists and ankles were imprisoned by padded clamps which had twisted their way out of the columns and locked themselves in place. Dr. Nicholas explained that they were operated by infra red and worked only when all four were detected in the appropriate places.

Now I knew that I was vulnerable. My heart rate increased rapidly and my mouth felt dry. He was looking at me with very obvious pleasure. He walked round the column on my left and I felt his hand on my arse. He complimented me on my curves and made me gasp as he held my right breast in his hand. But he did no more. Instead he came and stood in front of me. He told me that he would make a proposal to me that I was at liberty to refuse. He told me exactly what it was and dangled a gold Rolex watch and a thick bundle of £20 notes in front of me. I felt a throbbing in my throat and some difficulty in breathing comfortably. I paused and licked my lips. Without any action on his part I felt the muscles of my belly contract and a flutter between my legs. It was enough to make me agree, and I did.

He told me that we would be in the Cyclades the following evening and that certain of his friends would join the yacht. They would be given a gourmet meal, and then... I shook with anticipation of the events which would take place tomorrow. Dr Nicholas produced a remote and the clamps gently released me. I thought he was going to take me to bed, but instead he gave me a chilling warning about what would happen if I decided to change my mind. I saw another side of the charming, intelligent and powerful man who had engaged my attention and my thoughts from the time I first saw him. He seems to have everyone on board in the palm of his hand.

By the time I had regained my dress and put it over my head, he had returned to the warm and gracious man who I at first encountered, though, come to think of it, that was when he announced that Miria was to be flogged. I went back to the dance floor with him and he handed me back to Henry. I was rather agitated and asked Henry if he would excuse me if I went to bed. His smile was indulgent and also understanding. Miria was clutching Piers in the middle of the dance-floor. Even in the dim light it was clear that they were too engrossed with each other to be in any way bothered by anyone else.

I reached my cabin and determined to let you know what was happening, in case anything very nasty occurs.

Love and hugs

Laura

Dear John,

Thank you for your very prompt reply. It was reassuring to know that you have been keeping an eye on me since the beginning of the cruise. I am sure that I shall be all right, but the proposal was rather startling, though in a way it fell in with my own desires. I shall send you a very brief message tonight, though given the nature of the party it may be very late.

Love and kisses

Laura

Dear John,

I promised a message and this is it. At 7.30 I was in my cabin as I had been instructed and feeling very nervous. Miria and Venetia appeared complete with the costume I was to wear. To be honest, it looked like a pile of coloured rags to me. I had put my hair up, as I had been instructed, and made my make-up a bit more theatrical, but that was the limit of my own actions. Miria helped me into the costume which hung from my shoulders in a cascade of coloured streamers. It was a rather more clever than I had given it credit for, but it made me look shapeless, which disappointed me. At 8 p.m. I was due in the cabin I had visited the night before. The three of us stood at the door and were admitted. The room contained Dr Nicholas and five other men. They all stared at us but it was Dr Nicholas who beckoned me forward. I stood before him in my strange garment and waited for his next instruction. It was to stand between the columns. I knew this drill so that in a few seconds I was firmly secured. The men seemed to know exactly what to do and they formed a line to my left. They walked past me and each one reached for one of the coloured strips, gave it a jerk and ripped it from the yoke which encircled my neck. The first of them then walked behind me and pulled a strip from the back of my dress, rejoining the queue at its end. This was all quite harmless. By the end of the first tour I had lost ten strips of cloth, but there were many more to go. By the end of the second tour, my right breast and my left buttock were uncovered. From then on it was not long before I was stripped naked and was being surveyed by the five men with Dr Nicholas and Miria and Venetia sitting on bar stools at a distance.

The men seemed to like what they could see, which was all that I had to show them. The first of them stepped forward and gently kissed me on my lips. His breath was sweet and his lips quite dry. He took his opportunity to cup my breasts in his hands. His touch was firm but gentle. He held before me the six strips of cloth he had torn from my dress. Suddenly I realised what these signified as he took a cat o' nine tails from Dr Nicholas. He walked behind me and I heard the swish of the thongs as he swung them through the air. I tensed but he was not yet ready to strike me. There was another rush of wind and then the thongs struck me across my back, making me cry out and twist against the clamps. There was very little time between the first and second strikes. This one caught me across the buttocks, making me thrust my hips forward to the evident pleasure of the group of watchers. The third struck my right shoulder and stung my back. I tried to dissipate the pain by shaking my body, but the effect was to do no more than jiggle my breasts against one another, a sight which brought approving remarks from the onlookers. The fourth spread across the small of my back and the tips of the thongs bit into the side of my belly. I could hear my howls and gasps but hardly realised that it was my mouth which was producing these sounds. The fifth and sixth cuts fell on the underside of my buttocks, searing the tops of my thighs and then across my bottom to cross over some of the weals from the previous strike.

I knew that the man had completed his quota and I hung in the clamps, slowly trying to pull my legs together to find an alternative in my existence other than the burning pain of the whipping.

The next man was old but didn't appear feeble. He showed me five strips. He was quite tall and bent his head to kiss me on my neck where it joins my shoulder. His hands strayed first to my breasts and then to my waist where he ran them over the steep curve of my hips. It was time for me to endure another whipping. Dr. Nicholas handed him a tawse which was made of a double thickness of leather sewn together, about four centimetres wide and less than a metre long. He walked behind me and once more I heard the swish of leather cutting through the air, except that this was not a practice slash and I was unprepared for the explosion of pain that shot through my body from the bite of the tawse on my buttocks. I was gasping with pain and my inability to prepare my body for this assault when the second cut caught me across my right shoulder, to be followed almost immediately by the third which cut across my arse cheeks and left me shaking and crying out. I undulated my body in the hope that this would help to disperse the pain of the three strikes, but I realised that it was not having much of an effect although the group were appreciating my writhing.

The fourth slash was to the small of my back and the fifth was a devastatingly hard blow to my buttocks which made me scream and make my body into a bow leaning out from my wrists and ankles. As I was trying to become calmer after this attack I saw that I was being approached by the third of the men. He was tall and sparely built. He kissed my forehead and softly touched his lips to each of my eyes. He murmured something which sounded comforting, but I feared that this was an act and I would suffer even more at his hands. He held up five strips so that I knew what I would have to endure. Dr. Nicholas handed him what looked like a thin rubber tube. He wound it round his fist so that there was about eighty centimetres hanging free. I thought he was going to be kind, but I was disappointed.

The tube whistled as it swung through the air and I was ready for the first cut. This was not like the first two implements which were heavy enough to push me about, but the sensation was atrocious. It felt as if a red hot iron had been laid against my skin and it stung like a branding iron. My reaction was to leap up in my bonds and draw in my breath in a rasping gasp before crying out against the pain. Before I had a chance to recover myself he had struck two criss-crossed stripes which left me without even the ability to breathe, let alone cry out. His fourth cut circled my back and the end of the tube bit into my right breast. I could feel darkness welling up in my eyes, but this was nothing compared to his last blow which brought the tube up between my legs so that it filled my anus and my cunt with fire. I know I must have laid my head back between my arms and howled out my pain until the fire began to abate and I could look towards the other two of my tormentors.

I noticed that both Miria and Venetia were looking on with concern. Miria had her knuckles in her mouth whilst Venetia was finding it difficult to look me in the eyes. I was coming down from the burning pain that had been inflicted on me when I was approached by the fourth man. He had grey hair and broad shoulders. He held up five strips and kissed my cheek. He reached his hand to my breast and then slipped his other hand between my thighs. To my surprise I realised that I had gathered some lubrication between my lips and he rubbed his fingers between my thighs, partly opening me in the process. He stood back and looked at me. Dr. Nicholas handed him a delicate spray of birch. The ends of the twigs were fine and retained the small dark buds of early spring. He moved off to my right and I closed my eyes. It came as a total surprise when I heard the whisper of the twigs cutting through the air before they landed across my belly. I gulped for breath and then felt the sharp piercing pain of the innumerable biting ends cutting into my skin. I feared that they would penetrate into my flesh, but then I realised that although the pain was excruciating, he had not hit me very hard. The second slash was across the tops of my thighs and set me to try to lift my knees to ward off further blows. This was wholly ineffectual, but I felt tears begin to trickle down my cheeks and a gathering heat in my belly. I couldn't believe that my traitorous cunt was having its own reaction to the way I was displayed and the whipping I was receiving. Before I had time to take in what was happening to me he slashed me across my breasts. No one had ever done anything to my breasts that wasn't admiring and gentle. I was writhing in the agony which the fine fronds of the birch inflicted on my skin. But in my mind I was appalled that anyone could have struck my beautiful breasts with such indifference to their exquisiteness in shape and in their reaction to a gentle touch. I began to pant and gulp in air and feel a fluttering between my legs as I cried out in pain and protest. I hadn't time for very much of a recovery when he struck me again across my breasts and I saw them bounce and jiggle and small red dots appear from where the buds had been driven against my skin. My nipples were grazed and even after the rest of the pain subsided a bit they continued to be painfully and turgidly erect. Curiously, I felt less of this latest cut than the earlier ones. Something was happening to my body. I wondered if I gave myself up to whatever it was that these men wanted to do I would feel less pain. I hung in my bonds and received the last of his slashes which cut across the tops of my thighs, the lower part of my belly and between my legs to drive hard buds against the soft flesh of my cunt. I heard a rasping howl which I took to come from my mouth.

He had finished with me and rejoined the group. It was the turn of the last of my persecutors. He was younger than the others and had very dark eyes. He held up six strips before me and then discarded them. Unlike the other men he was dressed in an open-necked shirt and tight flared trousers. I was surprised to see that his feet were bare. He tipped my head back and kissed me full on my mouth. He held my head in one hand whilst his free hand cupped my stinging breast and then drifted down my belly to my cunt. They were practised fingers which opened me and slipped inside, whilst he used his thumb to locate and manipulate me between the upper part of my lips. He at once found my clit and from his pressure I knew that it was erect. I opened my mouth to call out against his intrusion, but as I did so he slipped his tongue between my lips and my teeth and I felt his tongue probing me as his fingers were lower down. I could do nothing to prevent him so I determined to enjoy his handling of me. The pulse in my belly became stronger, the fluttering more insistent. Such was his expertise that I wanted to yield to him then and there, but sadly knew that I had much to endure before anything could happen to me which would just be pleasure.

He stepped back and Dr Nicholas handed him a plaited leather whip. Miria had told me that this was the most feared of all implements that could be laid on my skin. I gave an involuntary cry and a shudder. He stood well to my side and I watched as he twirled the whip and then cracked it. Here was someone who knew just what he could do. His first strike took the little knot at the end of the whip into my navel. For a moment I thought that it didn't hurt, but then the pain came ripping up my belly and I howled. The second strike was to my right breast and I watched in horror as the tip of the whip bit into my nipple making my breast bounce and crease. Before I could register the pain he struck my left breast in the same way. I was in turmoil. The pain was agonising, but the cool way in which it was delivered left me in confusion, whilst the strikes he delivered seemed to add to the commotion in my belly. I knew that I had only to endure three more strikes and at least this part of my bargain was complete.

When they came I was utterly unprepared for the devastating agony they would inflict. They were rapidly consecutive. The first came up from ground level and struck upwards between my thighs into my cunt, the second brought the tip of the whip exactly on my swollen clit, the third buried the tip of the whip between my open sex lips. I had no sane response to this virtual immolation. I lay in my clamps and let my head fall back between my arms as my jaws opened and an unearthly howl came from my mouth. At the same time I could feel that my belly was knotting and tightening and juices began to drip from between my legs. I felt a pressure at my cunt and then hands on my buttocks. A long rigid cock filled me and I howled in agony and in ecstasy. I felt my juices gush and gather within me as the cock pumped into me. I raised my head to see who it was that was taking me with such vigour and was amazed to find myself clutched against the naked body of Dr. Nicholas. After the previous night I had felt that he had no use for me in that direction. I became desperate to hold myself against him and lose myself in the delight of his penetration of me.

I had not realised that the clamps were more than half open until my need drove me to try to pull my arms out of the bonds that I thought still held me captive. As soon as I was free I put my aching arms round his neck and drew his face down to mine as he continued pumping into me. I climaxed and then he kissed me and I could feel the pulses racing in my belly and my breath becoming shorter and more rapid. I opened my knees as far as I could and stood on his feet so that he could get the deepest possible penetration of my cunt. At the same time I grazed his chest with my nipples and breasts and within a few moments he had hoisted me up and then let me drop on his cock until I could see nothing but a scarlet blur as my orgasm took over my body and all my senses, though I felt and heard him as he finally released a long stream of jism into me. He caught me under my buttocks with his forearm and lifted me until I was well over his shoulder. He marched away from the columns and the group and turned into his bathroom. He kicked the door shut behind him and lowered me into warm scented water. He slipped in beside me and turned the Jacuzzi on to a gentle pulsing. I let the sweet soft water run over my tortured skin and laid back as he adjusted the controls and poured some liquid from a bottle into the water. He turned and held me under my arms and kissed me gently. I just floated into his arms and began to relax against him, closing my eyes in the warm scented steam.

I think that you will have had enough of this for one night, but there is more to come.

Love from the beautiful Mediterranean

Laura

Dear John,

I am sorry you feel like that about my experiences. I enjoy reading about what you have been up to, even if it does involve your ex girl friend and your cousin, to say nothing of someone else's wife, still, you have a large population to go at, whilst I have only those who come on board. Even so I have avoided over indulgence in alcohol, any indulgence in drugs and I have had a check up and I have avoided both infections and pregnancy. At the same time I have learned a great deal about what men like and what I enjoy, which to my amazement is very much the same thing!

You seem to have been thoroughly dissipated. How you and Charlie manage quite such serious and continued assaults on quite so many girls I have no idea. I must say you've never managed more than twice in one night with me. Either I'm much less attractive than these minxes you've been screwing or you were right and I desperately needed this cruise to set me free from my inhibitions and to realise what I enjoyed, needed and wanted. I agree I've certainly had plenty, but you'll be pleased to know that most of the weals have almost disappeared and there doesn't seem to be any permanent damage.

I promised to tell you what else transpired yesterday. Dr Nicholas got me out of the Jacuzzi and dried me off. He took me through to his bedroom and carefully lowered me onto the bed, covering me with the satin sheets. He sat beside me and told me all sorts of nice things about myself and then quickly dressed in a shirt and trousers and excused himself, telling me he would be back. I must have dozed off because I didn't hear him come back and it was not until I was aware of his body next to me in the bed, his lips on mine and a warm, gentle hand on my breast that I woke up and started to pay attention.

He told me that his five companions had been utterly enchanted with me, which I took as a strange compliment given that they had thrashed me so bitterly. He suggested that I might consider a new career for a while. I asked him what he had in mind, having no desire to be translated into the mistress of one of these men, however highly paid. What he suggested was that I should travel with him in his yacht and enjoy the company of the rich and famous all over the world. I should join in the entertainments much as I had done on this voyage and I would not only be guaranteed a comfortable all found living, but also an income which is at least ten times what I currently earn.

Dr Nicholas offered to look after me and my safety and security. I told him that I would think about it. He also says that I can have my friends on board and my mind at once went to Miria, Venetia and you. He says that after a year I can decide if I want to go on, or whether I will quietly return home. By the way, all costumes and my living expenses will be paid for and I shall see a lot of the world. So could you.

I'd say a lot more but Dr Nicholas, Venetia and Miria are claiming my attention.

Lots to think about. All my love

Laura

Dear John,

I am very disappointed that you took it upon yourself to rubbish my suggestion. You may earn huge sums of money, but I have little means of being financially independent. Your comments have made me think that I shall certainly go ahead with the scheme for as long as it lasts. Your unkind remarks have made up my mind for me.

You might like to know that Miria, Venetia and I will be sailing together. Today we started to work out our act for the entertainment of the current guests. Tomorrow we shall try it out on the audience here and ask for suggestions for improvements, developments and alternatives. I am very sad that we shan't be seeing each other again, though I realised that monogamy hardly comes easily to you, which is why you packed me off on this cruise. I am glad I made the best of it.

Tomorrow night is the last but one of the cruise. Dr Nicholas has said that he will make arrangements for the three of us to stay at the port, either in the yacht or in a hotel. I am looking forward to a few days more or less stationary.

Despite this break-up

love

Laura.

Dear John,

You will not be pleased by my final bulletin. Tonight the three of us presented our dress rehearsal, though that would hardly cover what happened.

We decided that we could have a series of scenes which might last about an hour and a half. In the first we dressed as witches and cast spells on one another. Venetia's spell meant that Miria became unclothed to the waist and fell in love with an oddly shaped log with which she attempted to fuck herself. I'm not sure she wasn't successful. Miria then put a spell on me and I turned into a bitch, very naturally on heat. Venetia lifted her skirt to reveal a large strap on dildo. She pursued me and eventually managed to mount me and shove the thing into me as I knelt on all fours. My spell set Venetia and Miria against each other and they wrestled with no holds barred until, stripped of their clothes, they found themselves with Venetia on top and Miria's legs forced apart as Venetia sank this formidable toy into her. This seemed to go down quite well. Both men and women seem to like women fighting. We might develop this into mud wrestling which always seems to be a turn on for both sexes.

The second scene involved a trial in which the audience was the jury. Venetia was the judge, Miria the prosecutor and I was the accused. The scenario involved an accusation that I had stolen someone else's husband. My defence was that no happily married man would find me attractive and that if he did he was not happily married and his wife was well rid of him. I wore a top which revealed a good deal of my cleavage. At the end of the extensive argument the audience was asked for its verdict, which was to the effect that just about any man would find me attractive and that I was a home wrecker. The judge indicated that there were several alternative sentences. I could be hung up for twenty minutes for the pleasure of anyone who wanted to avail themselves of my body; I could be given twenty strikes of the whip; I could be stretched on the rack for ten minutes whilst water was poured through a funnel into my mouth; or I could be hung upside down and swung amongst the audience who could do anything they wished to me provided it was not damaging.

I waited for the vote which was close but resulted in being hung up. That was not my preferred choice, but I knew that I would have to endure it. Spreader bars were attached at my wrists and ankles and I was hauled a few centimetres above the floor. In twenty minutes I had my breasts squeezed, I was penetrated front and back about five times and on at least three occasions simultaneously. I was made to come by a persistent elderly man whose fingers probed and pinched with more effect than his limp dick would ever have managed. Venetia called a halt and after a very short break we reappeared. This time Miria and I did our belly dancing routine as a dance of the seven veils whilst Venetia slowly plucked the veils from our bodies.

The last event was entitled the sacrifice of the martyrs. Each of us was stripped naked and arranged in a triangle suspended by our wrists. A number of implements were available to the audience who formed into a queue in order to whip us. They were allowed two strikes each, so they had to make a choice. If we managed an orgasm, the whipping was withdrawn from us. In the end the odds were pretty even. I was beaten across the back by a man who wielded a tawse. Though he made me tremble and cry out, I loved the admiration of the audience and the feeling of abandon that being naked, helpless and displayed gave me. The next was a woman who applied an unyielding riding crop to my buttocks which burnt as she cut into me. I wondered how the others were coping, but Miria seemed to be enjoying the admiration and the pain, whilst Venetia was squirming in a way that displayed her decorations in the way that the artist had intended. The third persecutor was Japanese who seemed intent on attacking my cunt. He had a plaited whip, but didn't use it on me in the way it had been designed, but pressed it into my cunt and jerked it in and out. Unfortunately he was vicious but inept and apart from my fear of him hurting me he achieved nothing. After that there was a succession of Greeks who lashed me across the breasts and an Iranian who took a five centimetre wide tawse to my cunt, but in a way that was both agonising and stimulating. I knew that this was to be the last of my torments and I pressed my knees together as hard as I could whilst I felt the sexual blush mount from my breasts to my face and the turgid pulse in my belly turn to a sudden stream of cataclysmic release. I vaguely became aware of applause as I hung, dripping from between my legs and utterly defeated by my own passion.

I had managed to have an orgasm after sixteen blows, Miria managed hers after twenty and Venetia spurted after twenty four strikes. There was much applause. In reality everyone seemed to have a good time.

So, farewell dear John, you have no idea what you are missing, though I often think of you.

Laura.

Dear Alison,

You couldn't guess where I've got to. Here I am in the Cyclades, island hopping on a beautiful yacht and enjoying a lifestyle which I had previously only ever seen in the pages of *Hello*.

I will tell you all the details at another time. You will know that John and I have split up. Though you wouldn't have thought so if you had been at Toulon ten days ago. I was walking through the market with two friends when I saw the Captain coming towards us in a beautiful black Bentley and who should be sitting in the passenger seat, but John!

I was amazed and stepped out into the road and stopped the slowly moving car. I asked John what he thought he was doing in Toulon and he told me that our Yacht's owner, Dr Nicholas, had sent for him to discuss a deal. I left the two other girls and got into the car with John. He told me he was sorry that we were no longer an item and that he thought of me a lot, and always as the best thing that had ever happened to him. I took this with a pinch of salt, knowing what he had been up to whilst I was away. We got talking and he asked about Miria and Venetia. He seemed very keen on seeing Venetia's adornments which I had described to him in detail in an e-mail. He kept harping on about getting back together and how much he really loved me and that it was all a dreadful mistake that we had split up.

I pinched more salt!

When we got to the yacht he went off to see Dr Nicholas and I awaited the outcome of the interview whilst sunbathing on the deck reading a biography of Spinoza. After a while Miria and Venetia arrived, complete with Prada shopping bags. I explained what had happened and they both looked concerned that I might go back with John. I told them that there was a chance, but I'd have to see if he relit my fires.

We had decided to join in the cabaret provided for the guests and crew on board so we went to the gym to have a little practice of a routine we had evolved. It was very hot and we stripped off to bras and thongs. In the midst of our rather physical rehearsal, who should appear but John. He made a fuss of me and then turned his attention to Miria and Venetia. He seemed very interested in Venetia, which was surprising when an almost naked Miria was present, and there was me, of course. I tried to shift his attention from Venetia, who was not entirely flattered by his standing rather too close to her and ogling what bit he could see of her tattoo. He had obviously had a good deal to drink and he crowded her into a corner of the room. I suspect that what followed was the drink working on John and her experiences earlier in life which could turn her into a plaything. Miria and I were amazed when John suddenly picked Venetia up, turned her round, dropped her on to her feet and then drew her wrists back so that she had to bend forward.

I started to protest at this treatment of my friend, but he's a big, strong guy and he pushed Miria and me away with a shove of his free hand, ordering us to just watch. I asked Venetia if she was all right and she replied that she was and she thought she could cope with John. He tore off her thong and smacked her hard across her buttocks. I could see the print of his fingers among the elaborate tattoo. Her buttocks bounced under the blow and the action started. John drew her upright and told her to provide the entertainment. She stood with her legs a little apart and moved her buttocks. John laughed and after a minute or so he twisted her round so that she was facing him. He made a number of obscene remarks about the snake and Venetia's cunt and then twisted her back to face away from him. In one swift movement he had started to push her so that she moved, at his insistence, to the bench at the side of the room. His wrist was round her front and his fingers were deep between her thighs. She let out a little cry and I saw that he had slammed her thighs against the edge of the bench and was bending her over it. He held her down with one hand whilst the other pulled on his zip and he brought out that big purple-headed dick I knew so well. He drew my attention to the shaft protruding from his groin and took it in his hand and rubbed it between Venetia's legs. I didn't want to be a voyeur when he penetrated Venetia so I looked away. I heard Venetia utter a howl of pain and looked back to find that he was forcing himself intro her arse, filling her rectum with that monstrous phallus.

If Venetia had been enjoying it, or had just been accepting, I would have turned away and let them get on with it, but he was raping her arse with demonic ferocity. Miria had her knuckles in her mouth, unsure, she later told me, if she should intervene in something which concerned my partner. I had no such inhibition and taking the pole which was used for opening the ceiling windows I struck him as hard as I could. The blow was supposed to be across his back, but he moved and I caught him at the back of his head. For a moment it seemed as if he had not registered my strike. He stood there with his dick shoved as far as it would go into Venetia and then he flung up his left arm and fell like the trunk of a tree. I didn't need to hit him again.

Miria went to the door and called for a steward. She told him to fetch Dr Nicholas and he rushed off. Venetia was gathering herself together on the bench and I went to look after her. She was shaking and tears were streaking her cheeks. I got her to sit on a chair and covered her with the dress she had been wearing. The doorway was quietly filled by Dr Nicholas. Behind him was the Master at Arms and a large sailor. 'Tell me,' he said. I explained what had happened and halfway through he turned to the Master at Arms and said 'Irons'. The bearded man bent and lifted John onto his shoulder as if he was no more than a rag doll and both crew members departed. As I came to the end of the very brief tale his face softened and he held my hand. He told me how sorry he was, but he had been taken in by John who had e-mailed him to ask if he could see me in the hope that he could arrange a reconciliation. 'I wanted you to be happy,' he told me, 'so I agreed to his surprise visit. I see it was not what he had in mind. Very shortly he will be removed to the quayside and he will know what will happen if he attempts to come on board or contact you. We sail on the evening tide.'

So here I am, an official member of the crew, with an opportunity to enjoy everything that these exotic cruises

218

can provide. And I have an admirer! I'll tell you more when there is more to tell.

Love

Laura

There are over 100 stunningly erotic novels of domination and submission in the Silver Moon catalogue. You can see the full range, including Club and Illustrated editions by writing to:

Silver Moon Reader Services
Shadowline Publishing Ltd,
No 2 Granary House
Ropery Road,
Gainsborough,
Lincs. DH21 2NS

You will receive a copy of the latest issue of the Readers' Club magazine, with articles, features, reviews, adverts and news plus a full list of our publications and an order form.